STRAVAGING "STRANGE"

RUSSIAN LIBRARY

The Russian Library at Columbia University Press publishes an expansive selection of Russian literature in English translation, concentrating on works previously unavailable in English and those ripe for new translations. Works of premodern, modern, and contemporary literature are featured, including recent writing. The series seeks to demonstrate the breadth, surprising variety, and global importance of the Russian literary tradition and includes not only novels but also short stories, plays, poetry, memoirs, creative nonfiction, and works of mixed or fluid genre.

■ □ ■

For a list of books in the series, see page 203

STRAVAGING "STRANGE"

SIGIZMUND KRZHIZHANOVSKY

Translated by
Joanne Turnbull
with Nikolai
Formozov

Columbia University Press   New York

Published with the support of Read Russia, Inc., and the Institute of
    Literary Translation, Russia
Columbia University Press
Publishers Since 1893
New York   Chichester, West Sussex
cup.columbia.edu

Library of Congress Cataloging-in-Publication Data
Names: Krzhizhanovskiĭ, Sigizmund, 1887–1950, author. | Turnbull,
    Joanne, translator. | Formozov, Nikolai, translator.
Title: Stravaging "strange" / Sigizmund Krzhizhanovsky ; translated
    by Joanne Turnbull with Nikolai Formozov.
Description: New York : Columbia University Press, 2022. |
    Series: Russian library | Translated from the Russian.
Identifiers: LCCN 2021049591 (print) | LCCN 2021049592 (ebook) |
    ISBN 9780231199469 (hardback) | ISBN 9780231199476 (trade
    paperback) | ISBN 9780231553148 (ebook)
Subjects: LCSH: Krzhizhanovskiĭ, Sigizmund, 1887–1950—
    Translations into English.
Classification: LCC PG3476.K782 A6 2022 (print) | LCC PG3476.
    K782 (ebook) | DDC 891.73/42—dc23/eng/20220105
LC record available at https://lccn.loc.gov/2021049591
LC ebook record available at https://lccn.loc.gov/2021049592

Cover design: Roberto de Vicq de Cumptich

CONTENTS

INTRODUCTION

CARYL EMERSON

Can we get out of here? This appetite has always fueled a certain type of travel literature, both real-life and fantastical, and Sigizmund Krzhizhanovsky (1887–1950) proved wonderfully inventive in it. At stake is more than the simple desire to escape where one is—although Krzhizhanovsky's private notebooks attest to his distress at being a "crossed-out" person among his fellow writers, his briefcase full of rejection slips. Feeding the positive real-life side of the hunger was his abiding curiosity about foreign countries and cities, none accessible to him after 1917 except through books or maps. On the fantastical side was his passion for Jonathan Swift, H. G. Wells, Jules Verne, and the mythologized eighteenth-century German adventurer Baron Munchausen, whose life and travels he updated for the Soviet era.[1] From these European masters Krzhizhanovsky took a particular sort of disciplined fantasy that he called "experimental realism." According to his lifelong companion, the theater pedagogue Anna Bovshek, this method first "borrows from reality," asking its permission to add hyperbole, but then "repays the debt to nature" by applying the strictest logic to the altered material. Experiments must start with acts of observation.

Since Soviet citizens had no rights to personal travel abroad—which Krzhizhanovsky was too poor to afford in any event—he dug deeply into his adopted city, Moscow, intently observing, tramping its sidewalks daily, looking for work and for literary themes. Between 1919 and the mid-1940s, Krzhizhanovsky deployed his method in hundreds of stories and almost a dozen dramatic works, from one-page sketches to novellas, comedies, stage adaptations, and libretti. Eight of them were published. With glasnost and the end of the Soviet Union in 1991, a way out for Krzhizhanovsky's creative work was found, first in a six-volume collected works in Russian, then in French, German, Polish, and for the English-speaking world through Joanne Turnbull's acclaimed translations.[2] No full-length biography of the writer yet exists, but excerpts from Bovshek's fiercely loyal memoir are included at the end of this volume, and they are a good place to begin.

Krzhizhanovsky thought in images, Bovshek explains. Condensed and logically precise, these images were always arranged by their author in relationships that led to a watertight conclusion (images must go somewhere and solve something: as Krzhizhanovsky liked to say, his interest in life was not arithmetic but algebraic). Unable to get out himself and without access to readers, this gaunt, restless, melancholy man was a "passionate traveler" who relied on new places to restock his brain. But whatever the setting, Bovshek says, the real hero of his stories is Thought. A thought is not a careless, casual, or carefree thing. It grows out of life but is better shaped than everyday phenomena, more obedient to laws. In the dark year 1937, Krzhizhanovsky wrote a brief treatise on the hyperbolic imagination titled "Countries That Don't Exist." In it he insisted that fantasies or inventions—the monstrous enlargements and extravagant diminishments of a writer like Jonathan Swift—"can never be based on nothing." When great wanderers (or young children) have an idea, they push it further and further, respecting its integrity, until it finds an environment worthy of it. Since available reality is so often inadequate to sustain a new idea, however, a country that doesn't exist is likely to be "the product of *impatient* human thoughts."[3] The three pieces of fiction in this book are nonexistent countries in this sense: two travel novellas separated by a catastrophe in philosophical form.

The first, "Stravaging 'Strange'" (1924), is the earliest and most complexly inventive of Krzhizhanovsky's travel tales of miniaturization, maturation, and loss. Its protagonist-Thought is spoken by a magus in the opening pages: the planet is cramped, we want a greater world, "but to greater there is only one way, through *smaller.*" Why should this be? The large route out is closed. We cannot physically board a ship and be gone across the sea, like Swift's Dr. Gulliver, in quest of old-type adventures. But we can always shrink down to an adventure, which is, after all, acutely vulnerable to scale. If we radically alter proportions in the world at our disposal, that world will become new and wondrously strange. In early Soviet literary circles, especially among the Petrograd Formalists, such self-conscious shifts in perspective were highly cultivated as a modernist device. During the war years, Viktor Shklovsky, inspired in part by his own disorienting experience in the trenches, had proposed *ostranenie* (defamiliarization) as the means to reinvigorate our perception of a stale, automatized world. Psychologically and artistically, Krzhizhanovsky was sympathetic to this procedure. In his 1922 story "The Slightly-Slightlies," a forensic examiner, whose job it is to detect faked signatures, suddenly wakes up to a world with its meanings "shot through with clarity . . ., slightly shifted, scarcely deflected, and strangely new."[4] He owes this epiphany to a kingdom of tiny little persons the size of dust motes inhabiting his eyes, ears, and pores. So happy is our examiner with his glistening new perceptions, which enable him to sense the potential for beauty in dead flawed shapes, that he declares an amnesty for all the world's frauds and forgeries. Dazzled by a sudden new angle of vision on a lonely, homely female neighbor, he invites her into his room for a kiss. But it doesn't last. The Thought-hero of this story is the delicate, temporary nature of enchantment. It's a sad tale overall, but one that remains well within conventional look-and-see boundaries of estrangement—and thus within the pleasure-and-comfort zone of the poet.

"Stravaging 'Strange,'" written two years later, goes further than the Formalist critic Shklovsky and further even than the fearlessly curious Lemuel Gulliver. The jolt of new perception might be good for art and for dispelling the boredom of the artist, but do we really dare to give up familiar space for long? How deeply and radically do we want to get out of here, when it's not just eyes or ears that do the work of estrangement, but our whole body? In Krzhizhanovsky's story, miniaturization goes far beyond what Dr. Gulliver experienced in Brobdingnag. First our protagonist is reduced to a speck. Then he is compacted even further. He can still think, feel, lust after his lady, get drunk, travel (as in: mount a red blood cell and circulate in an artery, or be broken on the wheel of the second hand as it rotates around the clock face of his mistress's favorite watch). His miniaturized size gives him unprecedented access to objects of desire or revenge. His rival, attacked from within, doesn't know what hit him. The cost, however, is that he is no longer visible to his beloved. The story is both harrowing and hilariously funny.

For the curious traveler, diminishment has its benefits. The micro-cosmos we thought was mute or inanimate suddenly speaks up with stories, once we get down to its level and begin to listen. Our stravaging magus meets a King of Hearts who relates how he was tragically affixed to the Flatland of a playing-card deck, all for the love of a woman (a deft political parable on the final Romanov tsar, Nicholas II). During his second journey, an even more diminutive magus is rescued from a ticking timepiece by a heroic grain of sand, veteran of service in an hourglass. The ultimate adventure, which takes place inside blood vessels and brain tissue, mimics the Russian Revolution. True to his method, Krzhizhanovsky arranges his images to evoke a recognizable chronology. It moves from the realm of a mechanistic eighteenth-century Watchmaker God through the hungry, vulnerable human body of nineteenth-century Romanticism to end with a twentieth-century proletarian revolt. As a fantasizer, Krzhizhanovsky remains a materialist—prudently, perhaps, for a Marxist culture. He has little interest in magic and miracle, but he is morbidly precise with cause and effect.

We recall that as *Gulliver's Travels* approaches its end, Swift bitterly escalates its misanthropy. In contrast, Krzhizhanovsky remains warm and vulnerable throughout: he plays with perspective, scale, and vengeance within unabashedly old-fashioned love stories, usually the longing for a woman, sometimes for a reader. "Stravaging 'Strange,'" from 1924, sets the precedent. "In the Pupil" (1927) will pile up rejected lovers in the pit behind a fickle woman's eye; in "The Gray Fedora" (also 1927), a leather hatband becomes the residence of a suicidal Thought that originated with a cuckolded husband but invades the brain of the lover.[5] These drastically reduced participants of tawdry love triangles exploit to the full the comedy of lovers' jealousy, adding to it the terror of survival in the uncharted wilderness, and ugliness, of a human body experienced close up. Once micro-miniaturized, a man is deprived of his familiar, well-seasoned toolkit of seductions—that is, his outer body parts. But he finds himself armed on his travels with more lethal weapons: invasion, blockade, an insurrection of red blood cells against white, a destruction of filaments in the enemy's brain. Yet, as "Stravaging 'Strange'" demonstrates, all the fantastical energy of these adventures is impotent to guarantee our hero those virtues at the core of the quest, which are recognition and love.

The second travel novella, "Material for a Life of Gorgis Katafalaki" (1933), differs in almost every respect from the first, except in its pursuit of readers and a reliable love object. There are no miniaturizations (only a brief metaphysical hallucination at the end), and the destinations—Berlin, Paris, London—are real. For a Krzhizhanovskian hero, the protagonist is singularly resilient: a person who wonders at everything, remembers nothing, learns poorly, constantly fails, is deceived and made fun of continuously—but who never loses heart and is never completely trapped. The Russian term for this innocent quality is *prostodushie*, simplemindedness or naïve good-heartedness, and it is often associated with fools. (Krzhizhanovsky is good with fools; two of his best plays feature them.[6]) According to the editor of the Collected Works, the odd figure of Katafalaki contains autobiographical motifs: an un-Russian name, uncertain profession, comic obsessions (say, with yawns), and behavior that chronically repudiates common sense. But the fictive character also embodies some of its author's unobtainable hopes. Katafalaki has a "healthy heart," he looks at the world through "rose-colored glasses that might fall off but never broke," he was a man who "loved life too much" to stare for long at dead things. The most obvious of these hopes was Krzhizhanovsky's persistent dream of foreign travel, especially to England. "Before departing for an unfamiliar place," Bovshek writes, "he would make a thorough study of its geography and history, its cities, historical sites and monuments." Among Katafalaki's wackier projects in London is to walk up and down every one of its eleven thousand streets, which—his pedometer assured him—would be equal to walking around the world "without leaving the city limits." He launches this pedestrian tour with some fanfare in 1914. The publicity stunt is forgotten by everyone (including its sponsor) within weeks of his setting out. By 1916, with "German submarines breaking through the minefields and nosing up the Thames," he is still walking. However lunatic he appears to Londoners who witness his obstinate stompings across their city, he doggedly keeps to his promise. At war's end, Katafalaki heads home.

The author's life provided some motifs. Also glimmering under Krzhizhanovsky's "material" is parody of a genre immensely popular in the Soviet 1920s and '30s: the narrative portrait of an exemplary person, drawn from all eras and cultures, user-friendly for a mass readership. A biography series, "Lives of Remarkable People," had been founded before the Revolution, in 1890, with precisely those enlightened aims.[7] The series was revived by Maxim Gorky in 1933 (and continues today in Putin's Russia, with more than two thousand titles). But Gorgis Katafalaki, measured by his achievements, is an utterly unremarkable person. His adventures in the European capitals are misguided and inarticulate. He cannot manage foreign languages. He bungles his way into and out of a duel of honor. In a tender takeoff on Shakespeare's *Taming of the Shrew*, he gets himself married to a monstrously unpretty girl, persuaded that it is his eyes, rather than her looks, that fall short. Unlike "Stravaging 'Strange,'" there is no sustained supernatural at work in his adventures, and hardly any plot suspense. Only at the end does the tone darken and open up to the fantastic. Katafalaki, back in Moscow and working as a dentist, is visited by Time. The new patient is suicidally depressed. Whole countries are meddling in me, Time complains, trying to skip entire years (as in Stalin's "Five-Year Plan completed in Four") or even entire centuries: "I don't like it when someone mixes up my seconds, much less my epochs." He is distraught that so many people in the capital speak of wasting time, or of wanting to kill time, and since he has lost all hope that he can hide from these malefactors, "take your pliers"—he tells Katafalaki—"and to hell with my wisdom, root and all!" The two of them take refuge in a Russian village, among a guild of friendly clockmakers. Naturally, Time gets in trouble with the authorities. The two travel novellas come together in the image of a ticking clock that can torture us if we hop on its revolving mechanisms. But we are not out of danger when we leave the clock alone.

What is the Thought, or idea-protagonist, of this material for a life? If its primary purpose is to parody the Soviet thirst for edifying biographies, then the sillier the adventures, the better. But Krzhizhanovsky provides another clue, more macabre and metaphysical. The name Katafalaki recalls a catafalque, the ornamented bier that supports a casket during funeral ceremonies. It is also the Russian word for hearse. One notebook jotting included in this volume reads: "To live is to put a spoke in the wheel of the hearse [*katafalk*] in which I am being carried." The idea is a simple one: everything that is born is traveling toward the land of the dead and life can interrupt this progression only feebly, a stick poked at random into the parts of an unstoppable mechanism. Still, that random poke is what defines our life, supplying it with its distinctive irregularities. As an artist, Krzhizhanovsky was fascinated with rituals at the life-death boundary. Some of his best tales are mythopoetic visions of the River Styx—receiving, rejecting, or suspending quasi-persons in limbo along its banks.[8] This novella begins with Katafalaki's death. A glint of light catches his eye, he fumbles for his glasses, but before he finds his focus, he has been knocked down.

More cerebral readings of this biography are possible. The Russian critic Anna Sinitskaya has taken on the one aspect of the tale that most resists formal analysis: the sprawling, preposterous *content* of Katafalaki's adventures.[9] She does not try to trim his travels down to an integrated storyline. Rather, she suggests that the task of this cautionary life story is to "realize metaphors"—that is, to personify philosophical abstractions by literally attaching lived experience to a random sequence of linguistic and literary clichés. "The entire plot is constructed as a chain of misunderstandings and absurd situations," she writes. Katafalaki might be a fool, but less of the folkloric than of the intellectual sort. He chronically extracts universals out of accidental encounters and nonequivalencies—and then looks on, open-mouthed with wonder, as the abstract and the material, the metaphysical and the physical, constantly change places. Sinitskaya pauses on a sentence from the end of chapter 9: "The idea, clinging to the edges of words, began slowly but stubbornly to clamber out of Katafalaki's head." This is the journey that matters. The "materials" for this life are not adventures in the sense of coherent ego events. Katafalaki has very little ego to indulge or protect. He can easily be distracted from a real personal insult (say, cuckoldry) by an intriguing phrase or abstruse cause that catches his fancy. This is why the travel plan of his life so little resembles a satisfactory plot. "In Sigizmund Krzhizhanovsky's world," Sinitskaya concludes, "there is nothing more ephemeral and illusory than the everyday reality of things, and nothing more palpable and tangible than a philosophical abstraction." The poor fit between these two realms—and our need to live *somewhere*—explains why Katafalaki learns nothing from his travels and behaves exactly the same in every place he rushes to visit. The reader "feels no resistance from geography," just as the hero encounters no obstacles while hopping from one country to another. Katafalaki, pursuing an idea or a word, is forever traversing exotic space and forever trying to join some larger community. But the world always ends up being only him.

Krzhizhanovsky, lonely and alone, loved to travel but instead found himself sitting on a boulevard bench while purposeful Muscovite crowds rushed by. Such is the recurrent image and authorial backstory. In an early essay titled "Idea and Word," written before the move to Moscow, Krzhizhanovsky worried about the fact that words had both a private and a public face. This boded ill for Thought. "The Idea isolates the metaphysician from life," he notes, "freeing him from the tangled mass of interwoven human self-love (society), and forces him some distance from life, in inactivity and silence, to serve only It. The metaphysician, in turn, isolated by the Idea, takes a word from the outside world and, freeing it—by means of 'isolating abstraction' . . .—from the tangle of associative threads, detaches it from life." Words that pass through metaphysicians are maimed; they "cannot creep back out into life."[10] Is this the good news for poetic creativity, or the bad? For Krzhizhanovsky, it was probably a reality beyond value judgment. But then this jotting turns up in his notebooks: "I would like to get out of my artistry (and my conscience), but can't find the door."

What remains to discuss is the philosophical parable that serves as a hinge between the two novellas: "Catastrophe." It is the earliest of Krzhizhanovsky's several stories featuring Immanuel Kant, for him the ultimate philosopher-analyst, bent on demystifying time, space, and meaning. Krzhizhanovsky, who was a gifted theater theorist, often opposed Kant (whom he read early and knew well) to Shakespeare.[11] If Kant tempted us with the Platonic folly of reducing the multitude of the world's things to disembodied essences, then Shakespeare was a practical master of multiplicity and incarnated matter. The problem with Kant's idealism was the problem of any solitary thinker convinced that a single brain had the power, or the right, to know the inner essence of alien things. The catastrophe is the revolt of phenomena against noumena—or the thinker's quest for noumena. In the nonexistent country where this parable takes place, Krzhizhanovsky makes bold to warn the world's things that the Thinker, having already contemplated the starry heavens and made sense out of them, is returning to Earth and about to meddle in *its* material, in pursuit of a pure space and a pure time that he can then store in his own mind. Panic, of course, ensues. Things do not take kindly to being analyzed. Houses take to their heels; alphabets flee from the pages of books. A conference is convened of all clockwork mechanisms: pure emptied-out time would be time without resistance, equivalent to timelessness. Again we sense a ticking timepiece, which can be heard under the volume as a whole.

In 1939, Krzhizhanovsky was asked by the Moscow weekly *Literaturnaya gazeta* to write a brief commemorative column marking the ninetieth anniversary of the death of Edgar Allan Poe.[12] The commission provided him with a chance to co-celebrate his own writerly priorities. Poe was an inventor of "psychological adventures, of extraordinary escapades in thought." He had a "passion for experimentation that stops at nothing." Unappreciated in his own time, obliged to make a living alongside pragmatic, practical, commercially minded people, "the American Poe lived in a country and in an era ill-suited to his attitude of mind." Sigizmund Krzhizhanovsky wrote those lines during a very bad year in his own country that, however ill-suited to him, undeniably also existed. Slowly he was giving up on his own fiction. "I'm a foreign tourist in life," he wrote. "It's time I repatriated to nonexistence." But his notebook jottings register a wide spectrum of moods. Perhaps all the same, some sort of survival was possible. "We all stand a little aloof from ourselves," he confessed. "I'm not on good terms with the present day, but posterity loves me." As Anna Bovshek wrote in her memoir: "it is not his fault that all his hard life he was a literary non-being, honestly working for being."

STRAVAGING "STRANGE"

STRAVAGING "STRANGE"

But this is wondrous strange!
And therefore as a stranger give it welcome.

▸ *Hamlet* I.5

"My watch says six. Your train is at nine?"

"Nine thirty."

"Well then, stravage a bit. It is so simple: to pack up one's things and to wander about in space. Now if Space were to pack up the stars and lands because it wanted to travel, I doubt anything would come of it. Anything sensible, that is."

My host drew his dressing gown about him and padded over the carpet's flat flowers to the window. His eyes, squinting from under ancient puffy lids, surveyed with compassion the space that had nowhere to stravage.

"Strange," I mumbled.

"Exactly! All railway timetables end by taking you there: to *strange*. What's more, your stravagings will turn you, your 'I,' into a 'Strange'; from the change of countries you will grow stranger and stranger, whether you like it or not; your eyes, once they have bowled about the world, will not want to come back to their old, comfortable sockets; only listen to the whistles of trains, and the harmony of the spheres[1] will fall forever silent for you; only scratch the soles of your feet, and they, itching to go, will turn you into a being who never returns."

I watched the bow-shaped lines around the old man's mouth twitch, and I thought to myself: this time will likely be the last. When I return, who knows how soon, I shall have to look for him not here—but in the graveyard. No talking to him then. I decided to force my theme.

"Teacher," I said, seeking out his sharp, even slightly prickly pupils with my own, "is everything they say about your travels true? Mere railway schedules are not enough. I would like to come away with at least a few words of instruction. My own experience is scant and dull. Whereas you . . . Tell me, teacher, at least your routes. Or your memories. Believe me, that *Strange* into which you say my stravagings must turn me will preserve every word, with not a letter out of place."

"You see," the old magus began, settling himself in a worn leather armchair, "ever since going to work for Co-op Fuel, I have given up even the thought of traveling:[2] let the earth fidget along its orbit, however it will—I've had enough. Most likely, the abacus bead too, flicked forever along its spindle, considers itself a true traveler. Yet its restlessness never takes it beyond the counting-frame square. Now . . . In my youth, of course, I had other ideas: then I always answered the summons of space. I wanted to go to the ends of the earth, to set foot on all the mysteries, to outrun the symbols and meridians stuck round the globe, and to probe with my own eyes the planet's rough skin."

"I can imagine. And I would like to have from you, teacher, the route of one of your longest and hardest journeys: the sort that captures the earth in thousand-verst[3] segments, that . . ."

"I'm afraid my very first words will disappoint you: my longest and hardest journey shifted me in space only seventy feet. Forgive me, seventy-one and a half."

"Are you joking?"

"Not at all. And I believe one can trade one country for another without resorting to even those few feet: for the last four years, my friend, I, as you know, have been hardly more mobile than a corpse. My window frame has not budged an inch. Yet that country whose people and affairs I—not without curiosity—have been observing is no longer the same country. And I didn't have to trouble about tickets or visas, as you well know, in order to become a stranger and to move from St. Petersburg to Leningrad."[4]

I smiled.

"Fair enough. But even so I must repeat my request: if not you, then perhaps your memory will spring into action. The story of your journey along a route of seventy feet should not, I think, take much time."

"Don't be so sure. Although, if I don't go into too much detail, I might just manage. What's the hour?"

"Six thirty."

"Now ... Perhaps you still have things to do?"

"No, teacher. I can listen until nine."

"Very well. Then sit down. No, not there: in the armchair. Now ... I'll begin."

1

"Today, having long since swapped my esoteric library for flour and potatoes,[5] I cannot show you, with book in hand, those complex formulas and maxims that guided us, magi, during the years of our apprentice stravagings. But the gist is this: the name 'Magus' derives from *magnus* (great), minus the letter 'n.' We are men who felt confined by the planet's cramped quarters, men who wanted here, in this small world, a greater world. But to *greater* there is only one way: through *smaller*; exaltation through diminution. Gulliver, who began his stravagings in Lilliput, had to finish them in a land of giants. The rules of our magic tutelage—since they meant to make us greater among smaller, giants among Lilliputians—naturally contracted the lines of our practice routes, leading us to exaltation by means of a long and hard process of diminution.

"The rails awaiting you now have always reminded me of an *equal sign* extending its parallels to infinity."

My teacher made a twofold gesture.

"But there is another sign. This one: < ."

Watching his palm carve the tip of that angle in the air, I nodded in silence and continued to listen.

"I well remember that limpid June morning when *my teacher*— this was forty-odd years ago—having summoned me, drew this simple sign of two penciled lines on a piece of paper and, moving his index finger from the left side of the sign to the right, said:

"'It's time you went: from here to there.'"

I looked at the line of my route and said nothing.

"You young men," my tutor added, "want to start out in seven-leagued boots.[6] But have patience: before your yard-long strides can become seven-leagued, you must teach them micromicronicity."

I remained silent. Then my tutor, with two turns of a key, clicked open the lid of the ivory casket on his desk and showed me three phials wrapped tight in cotton wool. Under their close-fitting stoppers, inside the bowed glass, liquids glowed dully: yellow, blue, and red.

"Now, this tincture," before my eyes the third phial, freed of its cotton, gleamed ruddily, "this tincture possesses an astonishing power of contraction. The contents of this bit of glass could shrink the body of an elephant to a clot smaller than that of a fly. And were one to obtain enough of this precious substance to sprinkle the entire earth, our planet could easily fit into one of those string bags in which children carry their rubber balls. But we'll begin with another phial."

With those words, my tutor handed me the yellow tincture. Only now did I see: on the label, affixed to the glass, barely discernible letters like tiny beads showed black.

"Directions for use," the master explained. "Obey these letters, and you shall become their size. Today, before sunset, this tincture must do its work. Bon voyage."

■ □ ■

In a state of great excitement, wavering between impatience and fear, I passed out into the street. The yellow flecks of sunlight dappling the burning noonday pavement would not let me forget the dozen yellow drops hidden in my vest pocket while biding their time, a time brought nearer with my every step. I walked along as if on hobbled feet: my imagination had begun to act in advance of the tincture; my steps seemed now strangely small, now unnaturally big. My heart fluttered inside my ribs like a frightened bird in its nest. I remember I sat down on a boulevard bench and let my pupils roam wherever they had a mind to. I was saying good-bye to space: to that familiar, azure- and green-painted space of *mine*. I watched hundreds of legs striding past: rhythmically raising and lowering their feet, bending and unbending their knees with a movement that recalled a steel yardstick confidently striding, to the jabs of a shop assistant's fingers, along an evenly unspooling bolt of cloth—they were unspooling and measuring their own familiar space, the space you see even with your eyes closed, the space you carry in you, lived-in and foot-worn, almost buttoned up with your body inside your coat. I listened to the friction of clothes against bodies, peered at the watercolor splotches of rippling clouds delicately inscribed on a blue ground; my ears caught every tone and undertone, my eyes every glint and sheen. I was saying good-bye to space. A rubber ball swung past in a string bag. I got up and walked on. At a crossroad someone thrust a newspaper into my hands. I unfolded its still-damp sheets and, scanning the columns, noticed at once the letters in brevier, like hundreds of tiny defenseless black bodies herded into lines. An association sprang instantly to mind; crumpling up the paper, I slipped a hand into my pocket and patted the cold plump phial. I had only to dash it against a cobble, to step on it—and . . . But this I did not do. No: it was at just that moment that my impatience overrode my fear, and I quickly set off home, past the clatter and glints, as if wresting myself from space. The only thing I saw then, with an almost hallucinatory clarity, was my teacher's long pale finger, which, having crossed to the far side of that broken line, the less-than sign, was beckoning me—there.

However, my excitement soon abated. I walked up to the top floor but one of the building in which I rented a room with a feeling of firm but cold resolve. In the semidarkness of a doorway at a turn on the narrow stairs, I was obliged to exchange nods with the neighbors who lived over me: our encounters, fairly rare, always took place here, in the gloom of the stairwell, which is why we never managed to see each other clearly. I knew only that that wheezing heap of lap robes, mufflers, and capes upon capes, jabbing the steps with a stick and scraping torturous soles on the stone, was a professor emeritus, if not an academician, who fussed with retorts and pipettes, with students' transcripts, as well as with his wife who, on this encounter, as on all others, rustled past me in silk skirts, filling the semidarkness with the scent of Chypre and the tang of alarm— and then, on reaching the top landing, waited patiently for the stick stumbling ten steps below.

I opened my door and, stepping inside, turned the key in the lock from left to right. I then retrieved the key and hid it in a desk drawer. The sun was sinking. I took out my pocket watch and placed it in front of me: six thirty. Now the phial: a magnifying glass, which expanded the tiny black symbols on the label, quickly and exactly revealed their meaning. Gripping the glass between my fingers, I gently turned the stopper: oh, how unlike the fragrance still wafting there, beyond the click of my key, was the rancid smell that stung my nostrils. For a moment I felt as if the old professor's asthma had invaded my lungs: it was hard to breathe. I went to the window and threw open the casements. Meanwhile the minute hand had described an arc of one hundred and eighty degrees. I had to make up my mind: I brought the phial to my lips—in an instant it was empty. After that I scarcely had time to stash the phial, in fulfillment of the will of the letters on the label, in the safe place I had fixed on beforehand: near the floor, between wall and wallpaper. As I was tucking the glass into the wallpaper crack, my body abruptly began to contract and collapse, like a burst bubble: the walls raced away from me; the ocher floorboards underfoot, expanding absurdly, slid toward a now limitless horizon; the ceiling soared aloft, while the flat, yellow-and-red wallpaper flower that I, while fussing with the phial a second before, had folded back, suddenly burgeoned, streaming like a gaudy inkblot up and up. An agonizing sensation made me close my eyes for a minute: when I opened them, I found myself standing by the entrance to a fairly wide glass tunnel with irregular round walls. Some time passed before I understood: this was the phial, which, evidently, I had dropped by accident at the last moment when I, now but a pitiful being the size of a dust mote, *could* still drop it.

On one of the tunnel's transparent cambers I saw enormous black symbols: in that same instant I remembered their meaning and my heart began to pound with joy. For the inscription on the phial explained how to return to one's former body and one's former space: I had only to find the magic symbol etched on the inside of the phial-tunnel's bottom and to touch it—and the reverse transformation would promptly occur.

I rushed headlong inside the glass tunnel: my steps rang out down the round sides. I ran all the way to the straight glass wall . . . "What if," I suddenly took fright, "the phial fell symbol uppermost? I could never scale that sheer and slippery wall to my salvation. I would perish an inch distant from the symbol: an inch would bar my way back to the thousand-miled earth."

But luckily the symbol turned out to be near the wall's lower edge. My eyes lighted on the two linked lines of the mathematical less-than sign. Having fallen acute-angle down, the sign was spreading its lines etched in the glass as a bird does its wings upraised for flight. "Freedom," I whispered, stretching out a hand toward the sign. "Fear," I heard half a second later. I did not repeat that word, but it sounded louder than the one before. Yes, the way *back* was near, an arm's length away, but I turned around and, slowly retracing my steps along the resonant glass, set off for the unknown *onward*. Then as now, I have always preferred and prefer the problem to the solution, the givens to the goal, the far end of the alphabet with its x and z to the elementary abc's: in this case too, I kept to my custom.

Minutes slip round a clock face too quickly, my friend, for me to indulge in a meticulous day-by-day account of my stravagings begun at dawn the next day. Recalling that from the floor to the window-sill of my room there zigzagged, as I had once noticed while tidy-ing up, a deep crack in the wall, I decided to make use of it for an ascent to the sill's plateau. It took me some hours to find the crack's lower ravinelike reaches so as to begin my two-day climb. At a later date, when I was crossing the Klausen Pass[7] with a group of alpin-ists, they marveled at my fitness and stamina; that I owed this to a three-foot crack in my wall, I, of course, did not tell them. At any rate, having worn myself out on the crooked crevices and precipices along my nearly vertical route, I, at last, toward morning of the third day, reached the window ledge. Setting foot on its flat surface cov-ered with geological strata of cracked white paint (those small fis-sures that I had barely noticed a week ago, sliding my palm along the sill, were now teaching me record jumps), I felt like a mountaineer amid the rubble of a mountain pass, surveying distant crevasses. The window casements, left open by the former "me," were letting in the air and, therefore, wind. I struggled against its gusts: clinging to the outcrops of chipped layers of paint, crouching behind their curled edges, it was all I could do not to be swept off the sill with the street dust that had settled there. Behind me was a precipitous drop to the floor showing ocher somewhere far below in my room, ahead of me a vertical brick wall, falling away into the fathomless crevasse of the street. To go on hiding in the cracks between paint and wood on the windowsill's dreary white plain would have been senseless and boring. I had to make up my mind: and so I did.

Clinging with a green paw to the sill's outer edge as it climbed the rough-hewn brick was some ivy. An ascent by way of that green twining staircase would, of course, be dangerous, but I, profiting from a sudden stillness, grabbed hold of some shaggy outgrowths on those living stairs and boldly began to clamber up. From time to time I rested inside the ivy's sticky crinkled leaves. But after several days of climbing, I noticed that the green landings of my staircase were smaller and narrower, while the spiral itself, after a few more twirls, dwindled away to nothing. Counting the brick seams already passed, I found that I was midway between two windowsills, three feet from the apartment of the old professor.

"Things are not so bad," said I to myself, swinging in my emerald hammock slung from a stem by a springy cord. "I need only be patient and rely on the growing power hidden in the ivy—and my staircase will hoist me up by itself."

So began my days of languid expectation: by day the sun, greening its rays, would steal in through the leaf's veins; at night I would approach the ribbed edge of my abode to admire the scatter of yellow and blue stars sparkling below. At first this transposition of the starry heavens somewhat puzzled me, but then I understood: the tincture that had shrunk my six-foot body to the size of a dust mote had also reduced the radius of my vision: my eyes could no longer see as far as Sirius and the North Star, while ordinary street lamps had replaced, as best they could, their constellations.

I often tried to picture what awaited me in the apartment of the old professor and his young wife. At the time, I was as young as you, my friend. And, of course, it was the vitality not only in the ivy's spirals, but also in me, that drew me up to the windowsill of the lady in question. Sometimes, on nights when I couldn't sleep, the bitterish smell of plant resins seemed tinged with her light but teasing Chypre. And while the ivy, stretching its green muscles, crept upward on tenacious paws, my imagination had already leapt ahead, into the apartment.

But when those three feet, spiral by spiral, were finally won and I, with a risky jump, scrambled onto the window ledge of which I had so long dreamt, I was met by an unexpected blow: a window pane and frame, carefully caulked and sealed, barred my way. In my youthful optimism, I had forgotten that the decrepit professor, even in the heat of July, went about under half a dozen lap robes and that the windows in his apartment were almost never opened.

Vexed and angry, I roamed for an entire day along a carefully caulked crack: nowhere was there a breach, or even a gap.

I could either: go back, down the twining ivy, or with inexhaustible patience wait for my *onward*. This time, too, I chose the latter.

Meanwhile July—I kept strict count of the days—fairly cool and damp at first, was becoming dryer and hotter. Suffering under windowpanes now scorching from the heat, I also rejoiced in that heat and prayed to the heavens for greater heat still: only tropical temperatures could force open the glass casements that blocked my way inside.

The oppressive days dragged on, separated by brief black slivers of night, also hot and humid. I was near despair when, suddenly one morning, glass and frame began to quake from inside shocks. Colossal clods of putty rained down. I ducked inside a narrow cave bored by a timber worm just before a rumbling shadow, showering rocks and lapilli, scudded past me. When I clambered out, I saw: the way was clear.

At first I felt like the man who has climbed up a rope ladder to the chamber of his beloved. Most likely that romantic feeling is what made me wait until dark. Slowly, step by step, shuddering and dropping to the ground at every sound, I pressed on toward the inside edge of the windowsill. I wasn't yet used to my invisibility; my every move, it seemed, must be noticed by the room's inmates.

That night as I sat with legs dangling in a windowsill fissure dreaming of my tomorrow, I was suddenly struck by a blast of air and covered by a gigantic shadow that eclipsed the entire horizon. Jumping to my feet, I looked up and saw two mountain peaks about to tumble down on me. In terror, I shut my eyes and prepared to die, but then a pungent whiff of Chypre made me open them again. Yes, it was she: the tips of two enormous less-than signs, so familiar to my mind and eye, clad not in pencil lead and not in glass, but in gigantic masses of bare skin, were resting to my right and left on the windowsill: these were the arms of the professor's wife.

For a minute, forgetting the danger and the risk, I moved toward the radiance of that intoxicating and humid living heat.

"What a warm night," rang out above me.

"Yes. But even so, darling, you had better close the window," something rustled, with a voice like crumpled paper, from the depths of the room.

"But the air is so clean: not a speck of dust. I don't see anything that could . . ."

"It makes no difference what you don't see, darling," the paper crumpled again, "some sort of invisible something will slip through, a bacillus, or the devil knows what. You won't see it, but it will seep into your air cells, your blood, and then what will you . . ."

The window clattered shut, cutting off my return route. But by then I had run as far as some bristling fibers on the young woman's dress: I gripped one of those fibers with hands and knees, and, heart pounding, waited for what might happen.

"There, there, darling, don't pout. Better fetch me the cards: no, not there, on the étagère. Farther left, farther still. Now then, let me see: damned solitaire never comes out. No matter how I play it: this way, that way. What did I tell you: again that king of hearts has muddled everything."

"If it won't come out, then give it up . . ."

"No-no, now wait a minute, I made a wish: they say that if it comes out, you must put the cards under your pillow and your wish will come . . . Heh, heh . . . Damn! There he is again, that fool of hearts."

Meanwhile I, having described gigantic zigzags around the room, was suddenly almost squashed against the edge of the table. Only a nimble somersault saved me from death, but the thrust was so great that my body, breaking away from the fiber to which it had clung, collided painfully with the table top. Keeping my wits about me, I raised myself up on one elbow from the table's yellow oilcloth and saw: whole flocks of enormous paper oblongs taking wing in a rustling rush, then sinking gently down on their red and black symbols. I realized what had happened: she had shuffled the cards.

This might have complicated the conversation, but just then from the far end of the room, from almost beyond the limits of my vision, came a third voice:

"Sir, oh sir, there's a student with his transcript here to see you. It's the sixth time he has come. What shall I tell him? Are you at home or not?"

From somewhere below I heard the noisy slap of slippers. Followed by the tattoo of her "little" high heels, as I thought, still unable to disconnect my ideation from the old circuits.

Left to myself, as I supposed, I set off for the chaotic pile of playing cards strewn about the table. A new, as yet hazy plan was forming in my mind. First I walked across the queen of clubs and, sticking out from under her, a scarlet lozenge on the two of diamonds. Then something black slipped under my soles: coming out of my reverie, I saw before me two fairly long avenues stretching away into the distance: there were no trees, only their motionless black shadows, strangely broad at the base and bizarrely slender in the trunk, lying on the snow-white surface of an oblong garden. I had gone but a few paces down one of those black avenues when I noticed that my path was twice crossed by the same sort of shadows cast by the same sort of invisible trees. Now I understood: this was the ten of spades. Its black patches could not, of course, bar my way, yet a strange feeling caused me to abandon those avenues foretelling death and to give that oblong garden a wide berth.

Here for the first time a foreboding, like ten black spikes, pierced me. Staring straight ahead, I walked slowly on from card to card.

Suddenly:

"Hey you, watch out! You stepped on my heart. Or do you consider it a mat for wiping one's feet? Get away!"

I looked down: by the rounded corner of the card onto which I had just absentmindedly stepped, a red heart, strangely flattened under the lamina of papery gloss, was twitching. Maintaining my balance but barely, I faltered to the edge of the heart and leapt onto the card's white surface. Now I clearly discerned the king of hearts' full red lips: ruffling the ginger bristles of his long beard, they quivered with displeasure and distaste.

"Who are you, outlander, to tread on me?"

"A man diminished," I replied.

"No diminishment is bitterer than mine," said the paper lips. "However sad the story you bring, the story you shall take away is sadder still. Come closer and listen."

Choosing a place on the tip of the king of hearts' flat gold scepter, I made myself comfortable and, stretching out my weary legs, cocked my ears.

"For my kingdom now," the paper lips began, "there is ample room even in that card box. My kingdom and my power were long ago disheartened: our venerable family became a silly suit, and I, who with my ministers once *played* people, I, now an ordinary card, must allow them, people, to play us, *cards*. Oh wanderer, can you understand a world in which miles have turned into millimeters, in whose palaces and huts the floors and ceilings have converged into one continuous plane?"[8]

"I can. Go on."

"My family—my father, grandfather, great-grandfather, great-great grandfather, and I—sat for centuries on our throne, surrounded by trembling and reverent subjects. Our feet never touched the dirty ground. Wheels, saddles, litters, sedan chairs, and the backs of chamber lackeys made our legs superfluous, while court intrigues and secret plots created a situation in which having only one head was not enough. You understand?" The king's palm, without leaving the plane, dropped down: I nodded. "As a result of the adaptation (speaking in Darwinian terms) of our dynasty to its environment, I, as you can see, have two heads plus zero legs. But that is not what caused the demise of myself and my kingdom. The problem was that in each of my chests, two hearts were beating: large and small. Here they are."

Without interrupting the story, I glanced at the card's gloss and bowed my head in acknowledgment.

"My large heart loved a little woman; my small heart loved a great nation. And both my hearts, large and small, felt cramped under my royal mantle. They beat against each, hindering each other from beating. This disturbed and tormented me. As it happened, a distinguished surgeon from the Land of Spades passing through the Kingdom of Hearts was then my guest at the palace. One day, having decided to put an end to my two-heartedness, I summoned the surgeon. He listened to me and to my hearts beating against each other, and frowned.

"'House of cards,' he muttered, adding a dozen Latin words.

"'But mightn't you remove the superfluous heart?'

"'Which of them, Your Majesty, do you consider superfluous?'

"For three days and three sleepless nights I agonized over that word *which*. But, alas, the nation that I loved with my small heart was far away, beyond the palace walls; whereas the woman to whom I had given my large heart was there beside me, beside my quarreling hearts, and able to shield from the knife the one in which she lived.

"On the fourth day I summoned the surgeon.

"'Set your instruments to work,' I commanded. 'I prefer the small in the large to the large in the small.'

"'But, Your Majesty, have you considered the consequences?'

"'The consequences to you, should you flout the king's command, have long since been considered by our laws. Obey me, or . . .'

"He produced his black knives, and soon I was lying on this very table, awaiting the touch of a scalpel. By means of a skillful transection, he removed my small heart, which beat for the nation, and placed it on the edge of the operating table, right here—where you see it now. I felt a stab of pain in my brain and lost consciousness. When I came to, I saw anxious faces all around me and the black doctor's back bent over his bloody knives. Concerned by their concern, I tried to lift my head up from the operating table—but that for some reason I could not do. The nurses, noticing my attempts, begged me with frightened and ingratiating smiles to lie flat: 'For now you cannot get up, Your Majesty. Do be careful, Your Majesty.'

"They managed for a long time, because I was so weak, to hide the truth from me. But when I felt somewhat stronger and decided, despite their pleas, to leave the plane of the operating table, I discovered, after a hundred desperate attempts, the terrible truth: I would never get up from the operating table because that *up* had been removed together with my heart; my neglected 'love for the nation' had gotten rid of me once and for all . . . But even so, you know . . . It would have been better if . . .

"In vain did my ministers try to help me: my acute flatness became chronic. Meanwhile my surgeon, in whose operating room six or seven of my subjects were dumped daily, cut out heart after heart and tried to implant them in me. Nothing came of this: he succeeded only in covering the white surfaces of his tables with the blood of sixes and sevens and nines. In the end, when almost the entire nation had been butchered, the vivisectionist fled and the business of trying to three-dimensionalize what is flat had to be abandoned.

"Thus the once mighty Kingdom of Hearts died out, while my disheartened glory and power fell into decay. But even here, in exile and diminishment, where the pomp of my royal levees has been replaced by simple participation in the solitaires of a professorial fool (true, thanks to me, they never come out), I have not lost hope, oh wayfarer. Here, in this flat box for playing cards, shuffled into a dog-eared deck, I await an intervention. Monarchies still exist on earth. And they will not tolerate the . . ."

"Your Majesty," I replied, "the disheartening by time is, alas, no less skillful than your black surgeon, and those rulers still ruling beyond your paper kingdom are also becoming flatter every day. They say the time is not far off when kings from the European pack, used to the amusement of 'playing men,' will be turned from those who play into those who are played. I'm not a pagan, but I do believe in Nemesis."[9]

There was a painful silence. Realizing that here was my chance to carry out the plan which, even before meeting the king, had begun to take shape in my mind, I went right up to the ear of that flat monarch and whispered into it with all the confidentiality of a conspirator:

"In any case, Your Majesty, I promise to see your memoirs into print. That is the only way we now have of making your words known to those by whom you wish to be heard."

"You have our gratitude. Ask whatever you like."

"I would like, Your Majesty, for the interrupted game of solitaire to come out."

His gold crown dipped down in a sign of consent. I hid inside the split corner of a card and waited for what would happen next. Before long I heard the footfall of the returning professor. His enormous hands strayed over the cards: I now soared up in the air on my paper plane, as on a glider, now swooped back down. Enveloped in the smell of turpentine and burnt tobacco, I was jolted about by the old man's trembling fingers.

Suddenly:

"Aha! Now here it has come out. Come and see, darling: it came out. But I shan't tell you what I wished for. Ahem . . . I'll just put the cards under my pillow and my wish will *come true*. Hmm-hmm."

This was precisely my plan: to steal into her bed. A minute later when, shut up with the king of hearts in his dark cramped box, I found myself between mattress and pillow, a sort of shame and regret took hold of me: the story of the king's two hearts and its sad end sounded to me almost like a threat. I recalled the stern face of my tutor, who had conversed only with my "large heart," and I realized that I had been brought here, under someone else's pillow, by my other heart, the very small one rubbing lasciviously against my ribs. A presentiment told me: only my large heart could deliver me from my smallness; the small one would lock me away in my present existence forever. But I wasn't given long to reflect: inside the box, suddenly swaying gently on the mattress springs, the air was becoming thicker and thicker with the mingled scent of turpentine and Chypre. The blood rushed to my head: I sprang up and ran to the nearest wall of the card case, found the keyhole—and leapt out the other side.

That's right. By the way, there's a switch by your elbow. It's rather dark: almost as dark as it was then. Turn on the light. There. Now I can see: you're smiling, my young friend. As am I: *now*. But then I was in no mood for smiles.

I hadn't reached the edge of the pillowcase when something almost apocalyptic began: the linen ground shuddered under me, its noisy billows heaving. Immeasurably huge masses of bodies writhed around me with menacing force. Feeling myself caught in a cataclysm, I grasped in vain at the edge of the cloth button onto which I had been hurled by a violent shock. A hot wind battered me from every quarter while colossal hulks of flesh and bone threatened to crash down and flatten me. Evidently, the professor was attempting to fulfill his wish. Nearly mad with terror and revulsion, now tumbling down into the troughs of raging linen, now soaring up as it swelled and flapped like a sail in a southeaster, I suddenly, in mid-career, collided with a moving living creature the size of an elephant. Under the jumping coverlet, it was pitch dark—but my outstretched palm could feel hard round plates on the monster's bristling back. At my first touch, it shot upward. Of all things, the fear that clutched my fingers to one of those plates is what saved me: together with the hard-skinned jumper, I flew through the stifling darkness, up and then down. Another gigantic jump—and now I understood: a flea. I clung trustingly to its slippery carapace and in two or three flights was past the cataclysm.

But at the mattress's outer edge, where my fabulous steed had carried me, the springs continued to groan and quiver. As soon as I had caught my breath, I began to let myself down by way of some silk fibers on the coverlet flung aside by the cataclysm. I wanted to reach the floor as quickly as possible. But a sharp smell of ammonia coming from below suddenly muddled my fingers, already trembling with repugnance, while my soles slipped on the silk—I lost my grip and went flying into the darkness. A moment later, branches like birch rods were lashing my body. Grasping at those supple boughs, tearing skin and nails, I crashed down. Something soft thumped the back of my head—and I lost consciousness.

I cannot say exactly how long my oblivion lasted. When I finally managed to open my eyes, I saw the trunks of a fantastical leafless forest, weaving a whimsical canopy overhead. In the wan daylight barely penetrating the dense thickets, I could see that the tree trunks ranged in color—from black to ginger. In some places they were translucent, so that through some trunks I could make out the hazy shapes of others. In the forest's sand-yellow soil, loose as if dug up by moles, not a blade of grass grew, not a flower: indeed this mysterious forest smelled less of flowers than of ordinary tanned leather. Its charm soon dissipated as I couldn't help but see that I was not in the enchanted forest of Armida, "temptress of the brave," but in the fur of an animal-skin rug by the double bed of the professorial couple.

Now it all came back to me. Oh, how fiercely I hated her then: if I could have, I would have trampled her like vermin; but she, alas, would not have felt even a tickle. Raising myself up on one elbow, I tried to make a more decisive move only to discover that I could dream neither of revenge, nor of immediately forsaking the animal skin onto which the professor's slipper might at any moment descend, flattening me into nothing. Yes, I was a too harmless rival.

But while I continued to lie motionless deep in that shaggy forest, my thinking took seven-leagued strides farther and farther afield.

Abstracting my situation, I began with maxims, so-called folk wisdom: well, "where elephants mate, mosquitoes will be squashed." From folk wisdom I turned to non-folk wisdom. I recalled a treatise by Kant on the Lisbon earthquake and Voltaire's remarkable meditations on the same subject.[10] Gradually their syllogisms took me beyond my narrow, two-inch horizon, and I, wiping away my bile and egotistical spume, began to picture the recent catastrophe on the mattress, whose victim I had so nearly become, *sub specie aeternitatis.*[*]

Aristotle said that society, mused I, is a "large person."[11] Very well, but then that meant that I, a tiny person caught so unseasonably between two undoubtedly "large people," was in the same position as an individual, a microperson, in relation to society, a macroperson. Yes, that day I nearly became an anarchist, my friend.

My health quickly improved, and before long I could turn from reflections to actions. As soon as I could get to my feet, I plodded off, still a bit wobbly, from trunk to trunk, searching for a way out of the forest. But it was not to be. Lost, like Dante, in a dark wood,[12] I at times began to think that I was near not the middle of my life's journey, but the end. Memories as well as premonitions tormented my tired brain. If I could have, I would have put it all behind me: the threshold of the building that had lured me, the limits of the city in which I used to live, the borders and shores of the country in which I was born. Instead, day after day, I wandered senselessly among dreary leafless trunks, powerless to get beyond the idiotic bounds of a smelly, dusty, dead animal skin not a yard long.

In the end I managed to reach the outer wood. I decided, while hiding in floorboard cracks from soles, to make my way to the threshold of the professor's apartment and to go back, to the phial. But I had not gone a dozen paces when suddenly I saw a new forest that, like Birnam Wood, was advancing on me.[13] I wanted to run back, preferring the inert forest to the one scurrying on its roots, but it, cloaked in clouds of dust, had already overtaken me. With an agility born of recent days' practice, I caught hold of one of its moving

---

[*] (Latin) From the point of view of eternity.

spires—and away we whisked, the forest and I, along a floorboard crack, in the direction of my thought: toward the threshold. Only when the flying forest had stopped just where I needed it to and I had picked my way down its sloping spires to the threshold did I realize that I owed the time gained to a floor brush that meant to sweep me, ahead of my thoughts, out of the upstairs apartment.

I cast a parting glance at the world of my misadventures and prepared to cross over the threshold. Just then a soft murmuring sound drew my attention. I listened: the murmurs turned into words. True, some of them stuck, like the keys of a broken piano. Convinced that the threshold was as good as mine, I set off toward the words, wishing to unriddle this phenomenon. As I neared the sound, I found myself in a pile of the crumpled cobwebs and dust with which I had stravaged on that floor brush. At first I could not make out the speakers. But then, peering more closely through the lattice of cobwebs, I noticed several strange, shaggy-pawed creatures seated in a sedate circle discussing something. They did not see me: the two nearest my eye sat with their backs to me, narrow backs covered with matted fur the color of dust. They were somewhat shorter than I. From their speeches, to which I listened with bated breath, it was clear that I had happened on a regular conclave of ordinary house Imps.

The year before, while studying folklore, I had become fairly well acquainted with the manners and mores of these tiny house sprites, who usually lodge in the cracks in walls and stravage with the sweepings from corner to corner so as to fill man's eyes and ears, his brain, and his very thoughts with the gray dust of boredom, disordering his work and disrupting his life. It is these Imps who, shaking their shaggy paws while nestled in the eye of a needle, prevent its being threaded; it is these Imps who, settled inside people's ears, know how to whisper lonely souls to death. There could be no doubt: it was their voices I now heard.

"The meeting will come to order," shushed an old hoary Imp, scratching his mangy bowed back with a round claw. "According to recent reports, our master has begun to smell like a corpse. A sure sign he'll soon be under the sod. So then, what should we do about his widow? I propose we discuss this now. Shirkh, you've just returned from an assignment. Have you been where you were sent? Did you manage to reach our mistress's lips and jot down her murmurings? People's thoughts, after all, like to be whispered aloud, and often in such a way that they themselves don't hear them. Well then, let us have your results."

In response came a long and laborious cough, after which the speaker began:

"The results, comrade Imps, are that my feet got wet and I caught cold."

A fresh fit of coughing briefly delayed this speech.

"The trouble is that approaches to women's lips are, as this distinguished assembly knows, difficult—there's nothing to catch hold of: not a hair. Wishing to faithfully fulfill my mission, I made my way to our mistress's favorite sofa cushion, the one on which she likes to rest her head when alone at dusk. After two days of waiting, I finally found myself on her face, but my perch, as it turned out, was under an eyebrow. 'Unfortunate,' thought I, knowing that from there to her upper lip was a good hour's walk. I had to hurry. She might leave the cushion at any moment, and then where would I search for her murmurings. I started briskly off, determined to get there in time, but as I was forcing my way through her eyelashes, enormous black arcs pressed against the cushion's gold embroidery, I got caught in a salty downpour. I picked up my pace so as to reach dry ground as quickly as possible, but . . ."

"But did you get as far as her murmurings?" the testy chairman cut in.

"You see," mumbled Shirkh, "when I reached dry ground, I sat down for a minute to change my shoes. Only a minute. The ones I had on were soaked through. And I suffer from rheumatism. I could not, for the sake of a woman's tears, risk my health."

"To hell with your health!" croaked the chairman. "Because of your idiotic change of shoes you missed hearing what you were sent for: her words. How dare you, you son of a snitch, appear here without a single one of our mistress's words!"

"Well, I did catch one. From a distance, it's true, and quite by chance. But if the assembly deems it . . ." He began to rummage with his claws inside a briefcase suddenly crackling with papers.

"We're listening."

And from out of a deathly hush I heard *my name*.

Many years later, I tried to understand how this could have happened: the Imp may simply have misheard. Maybe I misunderstood the Imp who had misheard. Or maybe . . . But why bother about all those maybes now? The point is: then I had no doubt. I felt a stab of joy in my heart. I must even have cried out or made a sudden move because the Imps fell silent and, bowing down to their toes, curled up like round bits of dust, blending imperceptibly into the gray pile of sweepings. Oh, my friend, never before or since have I experienced the feeling of limpid clarity and unclouded spirit I did then, inside that dirty heap of rubbish, when I, in pursuit of my name, calling sweetly and sadly to me, turned my back on the threshold and hurried off, pulling apart the cables of cobwebs barring my way, toward new adventures.

Of course, it was only by blindfolding logic that I could have decided on such madness, but I was drawn by that alogical force that attracts iron filings to a magnet and causes a stone to fall back to earth.

I was now in the vast, gloom-roofed square of the entrance hall, off of which opened three doors (of this last circumstance I learned much later). Here there were no sunrises and no sunsets, only the occasional flash and fade of a dim yellow star screwed into the zenith—in my former language I would have called it an electric light bulb. To get my bearings was extremely difficult, so it is no surprise that I confused the doors. Crossing over one of the three thresholds, I proceeded along a floorboard, unaware that I was not in her boudoir but in his laboratory. Only when, instead of dear Chypre, my nostrils were prickled by the acrid smell of mercury and alcohol did I realize my mistake. Thereafter I decided not to rely on my infinitesimal steps (oh, had I strapped a pedometer to my thigh then, I don't know that its drum would have had numbers enough) and to avail myself, where possible, of quicker means of locomotion. Given that the old professor plied, regularly no doubt, between boudoir and laboratory, I decided, mimicking the bacillus of which he had spoken with such fear, to use his body, like an old riveted steamer, for my next voyage.

However, recalling the Imp's remark about avenues of approach, I thought it would be dangerous for me to have anything to do with the soles of a shuffling ruin and that I had best install myself inside a cuff, say. But access to those cuffs could be had only from the surface of the worktable about which fumbled—among instruments, papers, and flasks—the scientist's hairy fingers. I decided to act accordingly: by now I knew a thing or two about scaling heights. I shan't describe to you how, after several days spent wrestling the vertical, I finally found myself on that enormous laboratory table. Metal and glass tubes gleamed all around me. I clambered up onto the lip of a huge vessel and saw myself on the steep metal bank of an oval lake. Bluish gray vapors swirled above; this was a mercury bath. A fierce headache sent me in search of other places to stroll. Soon my way was barred by a colossal glass tube with a rounded bottom like that of the phial which had abetted all my adventures. Raising my eyes, I saw that the tube was etched with black and blue graduations and numbers: perspective, diminishing objects as it does, helped me to understand that this was a thermometer. To my right and left, girded round by enormous iron rings, were rows of these same number-clad glass towers surmounted by glittering spires. No doubt this was where the professor conducted his researches into temperatures.

At first I seemed to be in luck: after two hours spent chasing the professor's hand as it ranged with a pencil over a notebook, I finally managed to jump onto a hair and climb up onto his somewhat hummocky little finger. But a minute later that finger had left the paper and was hovering, together with the others, over the glass tube of a thermometer. Curiosity urged me on. Clinging to hummocks of skin, I worked my way toward the top of the thermometer: this one had no glass spire ("Not sealed" flashed through my mind). Dangling from the hair nearest the glass, I peered down into the deep glass well. At that moment I had no idea that the Imps, alarmed by me, were shadowing the creature that had invaded their home—and that one of them was right behind me. Before I could recognize the danger, something shaggy leapt onto my back and dug a round claw into the hand clutching the hair. Groaning in pain, I tried to shake it off. But that only made the hair, by which we were both hanging, swing more violently, while the claw, lacerating my wound, rendered the pain unbearable. Weakening, I unclenched my hand and plunged down into the maw of the glass well. A burning liquid flooded my mouth, eyes, and ears. Still conscious after going under once or twice, I rose to the surface, catching in vain at the slippery walls. But the liquid buoyed up my light body, and soon, leaning my back against the well wall, I found a position that gave me some respite. My wound had closed almost instantly, without bleeding, while two or three swallows of the fluid on which I now floated had, despite all that had happened, filled my head with a joyful din and my muscles with a thirst for struggle: this, evidently, was an alcohol thermometer.

However, when the alcohol's first flush had worn off and my excitement had subsided, I began to feel symptoms of melancholy and fear. Then the drowsiness that naturally follows drunkenness muddled everything in my head, and I fell fast asleep, feet in the drink, head against the glass.

When I opened my eyes, I saw that the hole yawning high above had been glazed. I was all alone in a hermetically sealed thermometer. There was no way out to life for me, a dust-mote man: forever immured in glass, I could await only one thing—death.

However, death did not come—though that glazed vacuum should have quickly deprived me of breath and then life. The yellow tincture had evidently increased my body's death resistance. I had marveled even before at my ability to go for long periods without food, to withstand severe shocks, and, above all, at a strength (disproportionate to my then size) that allowed me to surmount seemingly insurmountable obstacles. Now all of this merely prolonged my struggle, without offering the least hope of success. The Imps, in whose affairs I had dared to meddle, were liquidating me: had I still been near the thermometer's fine glass spire, I might still have hoped to break through the thin glass lid of my prison, but here, down below, amid thick transparent walls, I resembled a fly hopelessly beating its wings against a windowpane. Yes, the black ten had exactly predicted my fate. The world was near, just beyond a glass wall, but I was forever cut off from it and excluded from existence. With agonizing clarity, I recalled the image of the woman who had lured me here, inside this glazed vacuum, and a passionate desire to return to that world—*her* world—overcame me: I banged my head against the glass wall; I pressed my face to it and scanned the hazy shapes outside for *hers*. But by my eyes there glowed only the inverse curve of the number "18." The thermometer stood at 18°.*

One morning I glanced at the glass and saw that "18" had increased to "20." An hour had not gone by before "20" had disappeared below and "21" was approaching from above, and then "22."† The elevator had gone into operation and was slowly conveying me upward. Now, peering at the glass dome of my well, I noticed that it was considerably closer. When I had ascended another two or three graduations, I saw a broad scratch zigzagging up the glass well's inner wall to the sealed top. Though the lower edge of that scratch (a fairly deep groove from my point of view) was still seven or eight numbers away,

---

* 64° Fahrenheit.
† 72° Fahrenheit.

a plan for my liberation, if only it were possible, came immediately to mind: I would wait until the temperature had taken me as far as the scratch and then, gripping its edges, climb up, along the zigzags, to the fine and fragile dome, smash it, and . . .

My heart began to pound from excitement. I tried to hurry the dilatory numbers. I couldn't sleep at night for trying to descry, even through the dark glass, a change in their red contours. Only two graduations now separated me from the scratch. But when I, having waited until dawn the next day to begin my journey to freedom, looked out, I saw, right by my eyes, a number I had left behind: the temperature was falling. Evidently, the period of sultry summer heat was over. It was already August, and now, as I watched the zigzag groove creep upward, I thought in despair that I could not possibly reach its edge before spring.

But fate continued to tease me: within a few days the shapes of the objects outside the glass had shifted. Around me long shadows crept, once or twice the thermometer rocked violently, and my body, which had fallen almost to "14," suddenly began to rise from number to number, up and up: the thermometer and I were apparently taking part in experiments to do with thermodynamics. As I watched the changing numbers, I felt like the traveler who, after long stravagings, returns to his native land and, gazing out the train window at the stations sailing past, waits for his stop with its promise of rest and joyful reunions.

I saw it, teasing me with its upward creeping zigzag, that accursed groove, I saw it almost by my eyes: another jolt, one more calorie, and my fingers would reach its edge, and then . . . But the saving boundary again began to recede. Containing my fury, I tried to calm myself, saying that the experiments would be repeated, that the old professor would drive me up and down the vertical many more times until I, sooner or later, reached the wanted boundary.

But the experiments were not repeated. And strangely: the movements of the shapes and shadows that had surrounded me ceased altogether. I puzzled over this, trying to understand what had brought the outside world to a sudden standstill, until finally a phrase from the Imps' conversation came back to me and supplied a more or less probable explanation. The professor must have fallen seriously ill, and work in his laboratory had stopped. My brain teemed with conjectures, one more dismal than the last: if *she* should become free, I mused, then how would she choose to use her freedom? And ought I to wait, in that glass sack, for my liberation by the spring warmth? Spring does its work not only inside glass tubes, but inside arteries and veins. She was young. We had nothing in common, save a dozen chance encounters on the stairs and by our entrance. We had never said a word to each other, save the one stolen from her by the Imps. And what could I, a man inside a glass vacuum, expect?

My nerves were stretched to breaking point. And when one day, as I peered through the glass, I saw an Imp who, clinging to an enameled number, was inspecting me with malicious delight, I could bear it no longer. I began to scream with shame and rage, but no screams came out: the vacuum killed them before they were born, and so I thrashed helplessly and soundlessly in my well.

Only then did I guess why the shapes and shadows that had loomed around me were always soundless: if *she* had come to me then and repeated *that* word, I, enclosed in airlessness, could not have heard it. I had reached that black boundary beyond which one cannot go. My thoughts stung me, so I decided to remove their

stingers: seeing no other way, I began to drink. I was, after all, floating on alcohol: I had only to bend down, and after a dozen swallows my mind would cloud, my thoughts would reel and dim. My
consciousness, before fading out, would flicker with bizarre visions
and imaginings: the smell of alcohol became that of delicate Chypre,
while many-colored dreams, as in Andersen's tale,[14] streamed across
the shimmering glass of my transparent dungeon.

On waking with a headache, I would survey the ever motionless
and soundless world around me and again douse my consciousness
with alcohol: soon you could say that I, without any metaphors, was
letting myself down: graduation by graduation, number by number.
Seeing the ceiling recede daily farther and farther from my eyes, realizing that my thirst, more unquenchable by the day, was dragging me
down and depriving me of my only chance, I tried to fight it—and
could not: the alcohol was sinking, and I with it. Inside my airlessness I did not hear the service read over the aged professor; and being
in my cups, I must not have noticed the funereal bustle and stir: by
then I was used to the alcohol swaying and rippling the shapes and
shadows in which I was enmeshed. I had lost the line between reality
and unreality. Thus I didn't realize at first what had happened when
sound suddenly assaulted my hearing and hurled me aside. I reached
automatically for the wall, but instead of walls there was emptiness.
Shaking off my intoxication, I looked around in wonderment: not
to the right, not to the left, not above was there glass; I stood on
solid ground, chest-deep in a pool of alcohol. An enormous block
of jagged glass glittered nearby, while my ears reverberated with the
ponderous tread of someone's retreating footsteps. As I learned later,
the thermometer in which I had spent six straight months had been
broken by accident during the usual removal and rearrangement of

things that occurs after a funeral—when one must somehow fill the emptiness left by that thing which was carried out, concealed in a coffin, away from the customary combination of things and bodies with things and bodies.

But at the moment of my liberation, I was little inclined to reflect on cause and effect: flung unexpectedly from death into life, I could scarcely believe my luck. Lest the glass sack close in around me again, I now walked, now ran, lest death resume its pursuit.

I now knew exactly where I was going: to the phial and to the symbol. I could already see myself in my large former body, I could already see my encounters with *her*, but on the way I would still have to guard against her soles. Were I to wind up, before my transformation, under one of them, I too would be swept out with the dirt and dust, unworthy even of those solemn rites accorded to the old professor's remains.

From that point on, my return journey went fairly well: I reached the threshold and found myself on the stairs. The steps for me were dangerous: instead, I descended by way of a steel sleeper to one side; its even slope and slippery surface reduced my travel time—down I slid as down an icy hill. Sooner than I estimated, I was at the door to my room. To reach the keyhole would be extremely difficult. After two or three failed attempts I began to search for another opening: thanks to a narrow crack between threshold and door, I soon managed to wriggle back into my old abode. Then a forced march of two days along the floorboard I knew so well—and I was again standing by the phial. I remember that by the entrance to that glass tunnel, much as I had longed for it, I hung back for a minute: after all that had happened, I was afraid to walk inside the glass: I might again be trapped in a glass sack. However, overcoming my empty fear,

I of course reached the magic symbol and touched it. In that same instant something seemed to explode in my body: ballooning like mad, it filled the entire tunnel, the glass walls crackled like the shell of an egg, while my body, still ballooning and ballooning, returned me to my former size and to my old space.

I took a step or two toward the door, accomplishing in one second what before had been a day's trek—and suddenly I heard the shuffle of soles and the murmur of voices through the panel. My first instinct was to duck down and look for cover, so as not to be squashed. But then, recalling that my transformation was behind me, I burst into loud laughter and, having fetched the key, went to the door. The whispers in the hall sounded anxious, almost frightened. After a minute, I put the key in the lock, but, strangely, its bit met that of another key inserted from the outside. On bumping into each other, both keys jerked back.

"Who's there," asked a faltering voice.

I calmly gave my name. In response I heard the sound of fleeing soles. Puzzled, I inserted my key in the now-empty keyhole and unlocked the door. Something on the outside prevented me opening it. I pulled harder—the door swung open, and at my feet on bits of string lay a broken wax seal. Evidently, my room, during the months of my unaccountable absence, had been sealed, and the commission come to open it had happened on the unaccountable absentee, who had entered said room through the sealed door. My serious former studies in both magics had earned me no glory, yet one silly incident with colliding key-bits sufficed to earn me the fame of a latter-day Cagliostro.[15] Yes, my friend, people have never known how to distinguish mysteries from hocus-pocus.

2

When I, a day later, encountered the woman with whom I had all but lost hope of encounters, we exchanged smiles and a bow. Her face was veiled in crepe, frozen snow crunched underfoot, but in me, ahead of the dilatory calendar leaves, it was already spring. And when, from under the city's thawed cobbles, anemic blades of yellow-green grass began to poke up through the cracks, while the blue stems of street thermometers rose to meet the sun—both she and I stopped hiding from each other those simple but eternal words, words which in spring, together with the leaf buds huddled against shivering branches, break through their dull sheaths and burst open to the world.

I was soon a frequent guest in the land of my long and difficult stravagings. Rather than wait, as one is supposed to, till worms had consumed the professor, we gave ourselves up to each other. This happy dénouement was hastened by the intriguing omniscience I displayed in telling my mistress, in our very first conversations, of all the most intimate details of her life, details known only to her, to the Imps, and to me. Much about me frightened her and seemed strange, but then mysteriousness and fear are one's faithful allies on the way to a woman's heart.

Time whirled quickly onward, and the hour hand sticking out of its curricle struck against the days with the speed of Munchausen's sword slapping, in similar circumstances, against the verst posts.[16] At first I gave my ladylove all my leisure hours; and when my leisure hours were not enough—I began to steal time for her from my workdays. My teacher frowned.

"I warn you," said he to me one day, "if the story of two hearts, revealed to you by my yellow tincture, has taught you nothing, I shall have to resort to the phial of blue drops. The power of contraction hidden in them is far greater. And the journey they contain is altogether more grueling."

I forgot my teacher's words as soon as I was out the door. And since I had let his words drop, I would soon be given the phial full of enticing but terrifying possibilities.

Meanwhile the sun-bright little world in which I continued to live had begun to tarnish and fade; my love, too, was daily becoming more anxious and sad. Her eyes no longer looked at me the same way and were not the same eyes. The clear sound of her voice was tainted with troubling overtones, the honey with wormwood, and the trust with suspicion and jealousy. Sometimes I saw in her hands narrow envelopes that darted instinctively away from my gaze; other times, if I arrived before the appointed hour, she would be out; once or twice, when we happened to meet in the street, I caught a flicker of displeasure and fright in her face. Her angry explanations were confused and overwrought. I loathe absurd scenes and even questions: I said nothing, but the gray web of suspicion wound round me more and more tightly, while dusty half-thoughts hung about on the gray cortex of my brain.

"Who knows," said I to myself, "if the Imps thrust me into that thermometer, then perhaps they pushed it into the hand of whoever dropped it and so freed me from my transparent prison." Yes, I could feel those gray shaggy-pawed Imps beginning to stir in me, filling my eyes and ears. And it occurred to me that only they, the imperceptible, were privy to all those imperceptiblenesses which, silting down in gray dusty layers, now tormented me and would not let me live. I, a being restored to his huge awkward body, had lost power over that elusive imperceptibleness wherein hid that tormenting *something* that turned every "yes" into "no," every "you" into "he."

"Well, then," I mused, "why not undertake another journey to the Imps? They know. But will they want to tell? And which had I better believe: those sprites or our lives, hers and mine?"

I remember that thought first began to smolder in me during one of those dusks when—as now so often happened—I was sitting in her boudoir, waiting for her light familiar footsteps. But she did not come.

I remember that in my impatience I got up and began to pace the room: my soles kept treading on a soft animal skin that muffled my footfalls. Suddenly I stopped, this too I clearly remember. I knelt down and narrowly inspected the reddish-brown fur, running my fingers through it. Memories suddenly engulfed me—and I, day by day, hour by hour, my face bent over the rug's dense bristles, relived the labors and thoughts of my bygone journey.

"Again I've lost my way," I whispered and got up from my knees. A new journey beckoned. Next morning I received from my teacher the blue tincture. It remained only to make certain preparations and to entrust myself to the future awaiting me under the phial's ground-glass stopper. From the uncertainty that had seeped into me, I was fleeing to the uncertainty hidden inside the blue drops. The time had come: to replace the pounding of my heart with the pounding of my footsteps.

My second start took place one day in early autumn. Outside the wind was tearing and crumpling leaves and flinging dust at the windows. I did not find her at home—the woman I loved: this, of course, did not at all surprise me. I didn't need any farewells.

In its usual place, to one side on her dressing table, lay her much-loved locket watch, an antique. Today she had forgotten it too.

For a minute I listened to its resonant ticking, recalling someone's measured and rhythmic steps, and then I thought: it's time. I removed the dial's fragile glass cover and made a barely noticeable triangular incision on the rim with a tiny file set aside for the purpose. Then I replaced the cover. Now I had my own forced entry to the dial's white surface.

My plan was simple: knowing that the woman whose solitude I wanted to study rarely parted with this softly ticking metal creature and often searched its face for her appointed minutes and times, I decided to install myself on the dial's slippery enamel skin and observe through the transparent dome all that went on.

Having performed the operation that collapsed me into a creature far smaller than an Imp, I easily found the triangular breach. By the time I stepped onto the dial, the hour hand, opposite whose tip I had filed my improvised entrance, had moved off, though not far; turning to my left, I could see it clearly, like a long black suspension-bridge extending overhead. The metallic pulse, reverberating against the glass canopy high above, boomed in my ears. At first the enormous white disk, across which I now strode toward the center, reminded me of the bottom of a round lunar crater. For quite some time it seemed to me uninhabited. But presently I was overcome by the sensation experienced by mountaineers as they climb up through the wafting, dimly visible, and almost impalpable clouds. I began to distinguish strange, utterly transparent creatures streaming past and through me, like water through a filter. Even so, I quickly learned to glimpse the coils of their bodies and noticed that they all, whether long or short, ended in a sharp, slightly hooked, glassily transparent stinger. A close study of the dial's fauna led me to conclude that the creatures flustering under the locket glass were *time bacilli*.

Time bacilli, as I soon became convinced, multiplied with every jolt of the hour, minute, and even second hand. The tiny nimble Seconds jostled on the second hand like sparrows on the branch of a hazelnut tree. On the minute hand's long black perch, their stingers tucked under them, sat the Minutes; while on the sluggish hour hand, their jointed, tapeworm-like bodies wrapped round its black steel arabesques, the Hours swayed sleepily. From those watch hands, shaken off by the jolts, time bacilli scattered every which way: easily penetrating the finest pores, they settled on nearby people, animals, and even certain inanimate objects—they were especially fond of books, letters, and paintings. Once inside a person, time bacilli put their stingers to work: victims of their duration toxin inevitably fell ill with Time. Those on whom swarms of Seconds descended—biting them invisibly like gadflies circling a sweaty horse—lived fragmented lives torn up into seconds, all bustle and exhaustion. And those . . . But your imagination, my friend, can complete the picture better than mine.

Before my wanderings in that watch-face land, I had thought that the concepts of order and time were inseparable: my own experience debunked that fiction invented by metaphysicians and watchmakers. In fact, there was more chaos there than order! True, almost every Second, say, having plunged its stinger into a person's brain, would dart away and slip back under the watch-face glass to live out its life in complete idleness and peace. But sometimes time bacilli, having fulfilled their purpose, would refuse to yield to the new swarms come to relieve them; they would continue to parasitize a person's brain and thoughts, aggravating old bites with their empty stingers.

Those unfortunate people were hard put during the recent revolution: they had no . . . hmm . . . *immunity to time*.[17]

Oh yes, my friend, several years later, working in my laboratory, I invested much effort in trying to produce for suffering mankind a *vaccine against time*. I did not succeed: does that mean that no one else will?

My initial plan had to be completely revised: what I had been searching for outside the glass turned out to be right here, under the glass. My mistress's entire past, though torn up into instants, was creeping and crowding around me.

One day I happened to capture one of those nimble Seconds. Ignoring its nasty clicking and ticking, I pressed it between my palms and peered inside its furiously wriggling body. And suddenly the Second's transparent coils began to bloom with shapes and colors, while its whiny ticking turned into the gentle sound of a long familiar and sweet, sweet voice murmuring, softly but distinctly, my name. I gave a start of surprise and nearly let go of the captured Second: undoubtedly this was that same Second, tracked down by the Imps, which for several days now had been leading me through both joy and suffering. Now *it* was in my power: I found a fine and supple filament, looped it around the Second's feebly twitching stinger, and began to walk it everywhere, as one would a pug or a lapdog.

My subsequent hunt for time bacilli only confirmed this phenomenon: duration bacilli, while injecting a person with time, would imbibe from that person *the contents of that time*—actions, words, thoughts—and, replete with these, creep back to their old watchface nesting place, where they continued to live like retired veterans or pensioned-off workers.

However, while I observed and studied these strange creatures, I also, in my turn, was subject to their scrutiny. My somewhat rapacious habits could not but displease them. Indeed, the annoyance I caused the natives of that watch-face land was growing only more pervasive. Of particular danger to me was the presence among those swarming durations of several instants that, long before, had suffered grievously at my hands and had spread ugly rumors about an interloper. As you no doubt remember, my body, when first affected by the yellow tincture, collapsed so quickly and contracted so abruptly that the time bacilli in my pores were strangulated and barely able to escape. These invalids were accusing me of a premeditated attempt on their lives. As I still had a poor grasp of the bacillary language, of its metallic clicks and ticks, I was unable to avert the danger in time, especially as time itself now rose up against me.

It all began when the tiniest of the duration bacilli—those that lived, despite my diminishment, inside me—decided in deference to the general mood to boycott me. For a time I was left *without time*. I have no words to describe, even vaguely and confusedly, what I experienced then, that feeling of timelessness. You must have read about that *thing* experienced by Jacobi[18] when, as a child, his mind collided with eight printed letters, *Ewigkeit**; it threw him into a deep faint and then a lengthy prostration after he regained consciousness. I can say this: I bore the blow not of the symbol, but of what it denotes; I entered not the word, but its essence.

The time bacilli returned to me, but only so as to subject me to the most barbaric torture: torture by durations. Reincluded in time, I, on opening my eyes, found myself tied to the sharp tip of the

---

* (German) Eternity.

second hand: my arms, bent painfully behind me, chafed against one edge of the hand's blade, while the other edge, digging into my back, drove me around the second-circle divisions with short strong thrusts. At first I ran as fast as I could, trying to avoid the blade's blows to my back. After two or three circles, I weakened and, bleeding profusely, barely conscious, hung from the hand, which continued to drag me past the divisions and numbers flickering below. The ghastly pain from the blade digging into my body made me gather my strength and again run around the eternal circle to the jeers of the gloating Seconds. During the Civil War[19] I once caught sight of an Ossetian horseman who had lassoed a thin-legged colt and was dragging it after him: the animal could not keep up with the taut rope, its weak and spindly legs kept getting tangled and stumbling, but the noose pulled its back and belly over the stony road, forcing it to run and to fall, to fall and again to run on its maimed and trembling legs.

The torture continued unabated: I knew that my mistress wound her watch every day, spurring the double-edged blade to which I was tied again and again. Then one day on my bloody round, a light flitting shadow touched cool black fingers to my disheveled and sweaty head. I looked up: directly over me—slowly floating like the flat of a gigantic sword—was the hour hand. And suddenly, amid the repulsively clicking bacilli, I heard a soft rustling voice address me in Latin:

"*Omnes vulnerant, ultima necat.*"*

Glancing in the direction of the sound, I saw, chained to the tip of the hand looming over me, a limpid gray creature of crystalline form,

---

* Every [hour] wounds, the last one kills.

its lively facets winking in sympathy. I wanted to reply, but the implacable second hand was leading me away from my unexpected interlocutor; and when, having dragged me round the circle, it returned me to our meeting place, the tips of our hands had drifted apart, making further confidences impossible. But the words of compassion dropped by the stranger had given me strength—to fight and to live. Until my next meeting with the hour hand, I had seven hundred and twenty full circles to go, and each circle would cost a good Golgotha.

The story of the little quartz man (we would cross paths for a minute or two, only to be separated for endlessly long hours) emerged gradually, coalescing from small pieces, like a mosaic from bits of stone. Here it is:

"I came upon this watch-face backwater the same way you did: by the power of fate. To try to solve her riddles is futile. Many centuries ago I lived in another world, one dear to my granular nature. It was not a silly flat dial, oh no. Together with crowds of other granules, sociably and trustingly rubbing shoulders, I was lodged in a marvelous world composed of two glass cones conjoined at their summits." (My new acquaintance had a somewhat flowery manner of speech, and I had a poor understanding of Latin phraseology, so I did not immediately realize that he was referring to an hourglass.)

"At first I was in the upper cone. There everyone was noisy, cheerful, and young. The spirit of the future lived in us. We yet-to-be instants, facets jostling facets, pushed our merry rustling way toward the narrow neck that marked off the course of *the present*. Every one of us was in a rush to get to that present and to jump, ahead of the others, through the glass strait. The urge to be *enpresented* seized me with an irresistible force: sinking straitward together with layers of other ambitious granules, I put my sharpened facets and relative heft to work, scratching and elbowing my rivals aside. Soon I had forced my way to the aperture. Edging past several granules vainly trying to bar my way, I jumped into the void. True, at the last moment, fear gripped my facets, but it was too late: masses of rushing granules were pressing down from above, while the slippery glass sent me plummeting. Down I flew and banged painfully into the top layer of granules sprawled like so many corpses in the depths of the lower cone. I tried to get up. I wanted to go back to that upper half-world from which I, in a fit of madness, had fled to this graveyard of expired instants. But I could not move: the chains binding me now are as nothing compared with the inertness and hopelessness that possessed me then. Lying with my facets stuck fast between the facets of other fallen instants, I watched as more and more of their layers buried me deeper and deeper among the living dead.

"I thought it was all over—suddenly a violent shock knocked our entire graveyard upside down, and we, expired durations, tumbled out of our upended tombs and plunged back into life. Some cosmic catastrophe had evidently occurred, overturning existence and forcing the perished and the yet-to-perish, *the past and the future*, to trade places. Oh yes, that false-bottomed world which I had to exchange for this silly black perch could do what other worlds cannot. And if..."

Here I interrupted the little quartz man. The watch mechanism had often separated our words. I was afraid my heart might give out before our next meeting: I had to hurry.

"That doesn't matter," I broke in. "Though your world is only a simple hourglass, I want to go there: where the past can turn into the future. Let's run away. Run away to your false-bottomed homeland, to that country of stravagers from this time to that. Because I am a man without a future."

By the time I had finished, the second hand had taken me so far from my interlocutor that I didn't catch his rustling reply. To call after him would have been dangerous: time bacilli were roaming all about. I kept quiet and, mustering what strength and will I had left, continued my race, bloodying the watch face with my lacerated feet. I lost count of the circle's black divisions racing toward me. A bloody haze veiled my eyes and my barely beating heart felt like a thread about to break. "This is the end," thought I in my dying lassitude— and suddenly I found myself lying flat on the enamel, arms free. Something gray and sharp-edged, gently rustling and pottering by my side, was trying to drag me away from the black lines.

"Quick!" the word rustled over my ear. "In half a minute the second hand will return. Buck up! Hold onto this facet: like so. Off we go."

With that, my savior—trundling facet over facet, like a tank— dragged me to the center of the dial.

By degrees I began to revive and was able, if with great difficulty, to walk unaided. From two or three harried phrases thrown out by my companion, I learned that the sharp facets of his quartz body had helped him to cut through his chains and that now we must hide from possible pursuit inside the watch mechanism. When I mentioned the triangular breach on the rim of the dial, my companion hesitated, but by the time we turned back, it was too late: long strings of transparent bacilli were slithering across the white watch-face field in an attempt to surround us. I could see them brandishing their stingers and soundlessly flexing their bodies: they left neither shadows nor reflections inside the glass dome and with every flexure were coming closer and closer.

"Into the mechanism! There's nowhere else," rasped my companion, fiercely shifting his flinty ribs.

"But how?"

"It's an old chronometer; pinion friction has eroded the enamel: let's try to squeeze through."

This I did quite easily. But my tanklike companion had to scrabble and scrabble with his brittle facets before the center defile was taken and we could both, clutching at cogs and screws, dive cautiously down into the mechanism's motive darkness. At first our eyes could make nothing out; but then a hazy crimson glow helped us to distinguish the outlines of steel wheels noisily grinding and clanging against each other. The glow came from the glinting bodies of rubies set in the steel: their spectral fluorescence guided us from cog to cog, often saving us from terrible blows rising up out of the gloom.

"Those flat-tails won't dare come in here," my companion snorted. "They can only slither after their watch hands, but into false-bottomed depths, oh no! And to think," he went on grumbling, "it has come to this: time, even time has been pinned to a disk."

I did not share the philosophical views of my friend from Ancient Rome. At that point, however, I was interested not in the metaphysics of time, but in how to get out from under the locket's snapped-shut back cover. Seated beneath the tremulous red beams of a ruby, we debated this question at length. I suggested we bide our time, then return to the dial and try to steal up to the breach. But my friend, not wishing to risk his ribs again, proposed a more ingenious project.

"Why not try to stop the watch? We need only pull out the hairspring that regulates all this, and then we, together with the whole steel shambles, will be taken to be mended: the cover will snap open and reveal the way."

So off we went, or rather rode, on the revolving cogs, now and then switching from one carousel to another. Their diameters became shorter and shorter until finally the smallest wheel of all brought us to that evenly breathing spiral, clenching and unclenching its serpentine body in the red glints filtering down from above.

"I'll destroy their time works," my companion whispered. Trundling facet over facet, he began his cautious approach to the coiled steel snake. I wanted to help him, but my solicitous friend, alluding to my still unhealed wounds, said that he would manage on his own.

I saw him bent over the steel's elastic breathing. He had already edged his sharp ribs up to the hairspring's metal clamp; he was shifting awkwardly about at its base when suddenly, unmindful of its movements, he was struck by a steel coil. In an instant his body, facets flashing, catapulted aloft, jarred against a sharp oncoming cog, and crashed down into the steel vise of the rhythmically breathing spring. But my faithful friend, even as he was dying, fought on: his body, now crumbling in the snake's steel grip, wedged itself ever more deeply in the constricting clamp. The hairspring, its convulsive movements slackening and slackening, twitched once, then again—and stopped. With a cry of despair, I jumped down, calling to my friend. But he had fallen silent forever. And death's silence, as if it had seeped from his inert gray body down the radiuses, stopped the wheels turning, the cogs clanging, the steel striking against steel—and the entire timeworks, clattering and gnashing only a moment ago, fell abruptly silent, leaving me alone in the stillness and the dark over the corpse of my only friend. Slowly, keeping an eye on the ruby glints, I got to my feet amid that particular "iron hush" later captured,

I believe, by the pen of one of your writers.[20] On reaching the concave bottom of the stopped chronometer's back cover, I had to cool my heels for another day or two before it was snapped open. With the first shock of the sun's rays, I, squinting against the light, jumped quickly out.

My conjectures proved correct: I was on a watchmaker's worktable and a minute after my liberation had to hide from the lens of his hovering loupe: to be noticed by the watchmaker was not, of course, part of my plan.

Trying to remain not far from my mistress's locket watch, I waited until it had been set going again, then hid deep inside a gold notch on the winding knob. Once or twice I was made to spin around, curled up in a ball under the watchmaker's acrid fingers. But soon I detected a familiar teasing fragrance and scrambled out of my refuge. Directly over me was the corneous canopy of a translucent fingernail: leaping up and falling back down, I at last managed to clamber into a crack between skin and nail of my girlfriend, where a paroxysm of happiness at our reunion made me weep. All the verses in the Song of Songs[21] could not convey the feeling produced in me by nearness to my inamorata. Even if her fragrant fingers, in turning the winding knob, had condemned me to another bloody Golgotha, even if her springy nail could crush me like a pitiful gnat, I blessed those sufferings and that death, because both death and sufferings came from *her*. And when, as if in answer to my happiness, a steel blade suddenly flashed overhead and cut into the fingernail from whose tip I dangled ("Scissors," sprang to mind), I felt not a moment's fear or rage. Pared away with that sliver of nail, I plunged resignedly down.

Fortunately, to the soft table cloth onto which I fell was not far: I escaped without a bruise.

Oh, my dear fellow, if someone were to claim now that my entire library, exchanged for half-frozen potatoes, wasn't worth even a potato peeling, I would hardly argue, but if you were to insist that the magic hidden in love is merely the invention of fools and poets, why then . . . I also wouldn't argue with you, but I would know for a fact that you had yet to understand love: for it is two whole magics—black and white—coexisting like the black and white squares on a chessboard. And to finish with this comparison, I, in my stravaging days, was more like a chessman, lost in the black-and-white maze, than a chess player.

But to return: to embrace a sliver of my mistress's fingernail was by then not enough, I wanted all of her and, seized by a yearning to return, made straight for the phial, hidden, as I clearly recalled, right there on the table, under the inkpot's metal concavity. It was then that I came across a black square on love's chessboard: strangely, it looked like a white paper square quietly barring my way. Chary of my minutes, I decided not to change course and stepped boldly onto the white square. In that same second, enormous black symbols—spilling one from another with a scratchy sound along the paper's blue paths—came caracoling toward me. I leapt aside just in time and, when the symbols had rushed past at the speed of an express train on blue rails, continued on my way, keeping to one side of the still-wet inky whorls: letter by letter they were forming a funny abracadabra, but when I put them together in reverse order, I didn't feel like laughing. I faced about and raced after the runaway words, devouring with my eyes their increasingly—word by word—ominous meaning. According to Bely, if a word begins with "l-o,"[22] it's not yet clear what's next: "love" or "lotus." Yet having run as far as that "l-o," I suddenly felt my legs give way. Wiping cold sweat from my face, I sank down onto the paper: I was inscribed, as if in a vicious circle, in the small black zero of the final cursive "e." In that agonizing moment, I imagined that the whole world, as diminished as I, ended there: inside that tight inky noose.

While I was sitting there, a white rustling ceiling swooped down on the missive. Before I could realize what was happening and take measures, I found myself inside a sealed envelope with my rival's name written somewhere on the outside of that solid paper mass. In my fury, I began dashing about, but it was useless and only led to my stumbling, in the envelope's semidarkness, upon more and more words, stuck to the paper in high relief. I couldn't help but interpret them, which caused me fresh pain. When I had done raving, I skulked in a corner of the envelope and began to wait for what would happen next.

Alas, I had more than enough time for reflection. The address hidden from my eyes spirited the letter over a distance of hundreds of versts. I realized that for me now, a man smaller than a dust mote, to go back to the saving glass zigzag would be as easy as for inhabitants of the Dog Star to reach our Earth. At times I took bitter delight in comparing myself to a tiny male butterfly of the genus Vanessa,[23] lured by nature to the mandibles of his giganticized girlfriend, threaded through all the secrets of her body, and then expelled together with her excrement.

My thoughts dragged on—as did my journey. The envelope's paper sheath was a poor defense against the icy cold that tormented me in the street mailbox and for part of the route: lurching about inside my own dark and unheated freight car, I toughened myself for those stravagings later forced on us by the hard and hungry years of wars.[24]

A few days went by, and then the hand of the addressee opened the envelope. Oh, how I loathed my liberator: even before I encountered him, or rather his cuff, which came right up to me as the letter was being read. I was now an experienced climber—and it cost me nothing, having jumped onto that cuff, to hike to the yellow hummocks of his skin and then up through the sparse ginger underbrush on the slopes of his arm to the sheer white crater of his high stiff collar from where, profiting by the dermal gullies and pimply hillocks, I proceeded by easy stages to the bristly moustache overhanging the red funnel of his mouth. In this case, the Imps' practice of intercepting whispers struck me as perfectly appropriate.

However, nothing came of my endeavor: air either rumbling or mumbling kept rushing past me, while no whir of whispers ever materialized. At the same time, the locale was in constant turmoil: the mouth of this monster was always working: now smacking its lips against other lips, now sucking on a shot glass or a wineglass, now quivering and twitching from loud laughter and rapid-fire words. I am no Leporello[25] and so kept no catalogue of the kisses that gave me no peace, especially at night when I, only half-awake, had to hold on tight to my lookout whisker so as not go tumbling down between lips and lips. Exhausted by my difficult journey and want of sleep, worn out by my abiding humiliation and hatred for this dirty, absurdly huge animal, sought out from hundreds of versts away by the words of *her* declarations, I could no longer bear the thought that my gargantuan rival was alive and apparently had no intention of not living.

But what could I do? For a start, I decided to make a reconnaissance. Snatching an hour when the monster had begun to snore, I climbed down from my lookout post, clambered through the half-open lips and over the crevasse of a crumbling filling to the surface of his tongue: a tussocky morass squelching with slime and ooze that kept slopping over my feet. Step-by-step, from tussock to tussock, I made my way to his palate and, before the monster could close his jaw, negotiated the narrow, catacomb-like Eustachian tube. On reaching the middle ear, I made my way down a short passage— breaking through the mesh of tissue that blocked my way in just one place—to the organ of Corti: five and a half more rings and that spiral structure might have been a model of Dante's hell. By this time the monster had awoken and the sounds of his voice winding their way into that resonant organ caught my ear with particular importunity. I began to consider what course to pursue. By chance I recalled the "hypothetical homunculus" invented by Leibniz[26] in a letter to Coste:[27] this hypothetical homunculus, admitted for polemical purposes inside a man's brain, among whose cells he freely roams, returns—as that metaphysician's mathematical imagination would have it—with a whole heap of arguments supposedly disproving materialism.[28] My situation did not dispose me to philosophize, and if I wanted to disprove anything, then only the right to existence enjoyed by the creature in whose tissues I found myself. Yet Leibniz's phantasm appealed to me: I decided it was time, high time, that phantasm went from myth to reality.

Soon I was picking my way among branching dendrites and neurons that had entangled their axial shoots in a single brainpan. The Florentine's mournful shade, companion to all parted lovers, recalled to me his canto describing the Wood of Suicides:[29] the neural branches were alive and stirring, they recoiled at my touch and, when I tore them apart, their fibrils oozed blood and sticky moisture.

I was inside the mind of my enemy: I could see the quivering and shriveling of loose associative threads; with curiosity I observed the tentacles of nerve cells now retracting, now extending, coupling and uncoupling their long vibrating extremities. I began to take charge of this other man's brain in the manner of a savage faced with a telephone switchboard: I ripped apart associative filaments as one rips out wires in the enemy's rear; I mangled the ends of neurons, at least the ones I could manage. Some sinuous nerve branches that recoiled from one another, I forcibly tied together with a double fisherman's knot. If I could have, I would have uprooted that whole thinking forest, but I was too small and weak and soon, dead tired, spattered with blood and bits of brain, I abandoned my cruel but useless work. While I rested, the living forest sprouted new threads and, enmeshing me in thousands upon thousands of cells, went on with the coupling and uncoupling of its branches, the creep and quiver of its fine and slimy white and gray tangles.

Working alone, with just my two hands, I could do nothing: I needed the collective efforts of hundreds upon hundreds like me. Meanwhile my adversary, no doubt calmly receiving all these vibrations in the form of so-called life, did not suspect that into his mind had stolen another mind hostile to his own, one whose entire logic and power were bent on destroying him forever. Yes, the dust mote wanted to demolish the mountain, to pitch it down into nothingness. If David with his flimsy sling could slay a giant,[30] then why couldn't my vengeance, thought I, besiege a giant thousands of times larger. True, the biblical fighter had a certain advantage over me in size, but then I had the advantage of my position. Without a moment's delay, I set about preparing my attack.

To begin with, I must infiltrate the enemy's blood. I tore open a nearby capillary and, propelled by the bloodstream, slid swiftly along broader and broader veins toward his heart. Gliding along beside me—now banding together, now scattering, while bumping into walls—were some fairly large, ring-shaped creatures whose distended sides sucked in and squeezed out blood. Sometimes these porous sacks would rub against each other with their ribbed rings: this was the silent language in which these red flatfish, as I initially called them, communicated among themselves; later I realized they were simply red blood cells.

Straddling the moving sides of one of these creatures, I skimmed along with relative ease between the round walls of arteries. At first the disgruntled creature shook its sides, trying to throw me into the bloodstream, but then we became used to one another. Sitting astride one of the ribs on that ring, the living tissue that enveloped the body of my steed, I noticed that he, unlike the other round creatures in our midst, was trying to swim against the current, which greatly slowed our progress. But when an accidental jolt shifted me to another rib on the ring, my steed immediately started swimming in the opposite direction. Thereafter I shifted from rib to rib systematically, bearing down with my full weight—and every time the red sack altered its course: thus I began to master the living language of red blood cells. It proved rich enough to absorb what was taking shape ever more clearly in my mind. David's sling extended his arm, in the unequal contest he fought, by only a couple of cubits. Whereas I wanted to unleash a sling that could deliver a strike to the most distant targets, a sling tested and proven over centuries of struggle: I mean *agitation*.

Bearing down, like a pianist on the keys of a piano, on the ribs of multitudes of living rings swimming past in the perpetual bloodstream, I played, displaying rather good finger technique, my *Totentanz*,* after which I had to slam the black lid down on that entire keyboard forever. Inside the gigantic factory where I now was, the pumps and valves functioned without pause, while the wretched blood workers were driven along veins and arteries by the heart's never-ceasing jolts. Day and night those round toilers circled from heart to lungs and back again. Having unloaded their tanks of oxygen, they would creep away, turning black from the strain, under their burdens of carbon dioxide and hemoglobin. It never entered their heads . . . Beg pardon, they none of them had a head—whereas I did—the thought never occurred to their ribbed rings that the organization of their labor was based on principles of exploitation.

I had to touch thousands upon thousands of the ribs rubbing against me before those rancor-absorbing sacks took to my idea of a Veinsters Union and an eight-hour workday. The idea of somehow doing away with the monster tormenting both me and them, poor voiceless round-the-clock workers, now obsessed me. Had some latter-day Menenius Agrippa[31] entered our midst, he could not have dissuaded—with his idiotic fables—either me, tribune of the circulatory plebs, or my best disciples, who, rubbing their eloquent ribs against all living rings in their path, whirled along every branching of the bloodstream, delivering to all parts our slogan: EIGHT HOURS CIRCULATION A DAY! AND NOT A SECOND MORE!

I did not dismount for an instant from the ribbed back of my new friend, who taught me not only the language of red blood cells but a warmhearted feeling for them; this feeling strengthened with every beat of a heart that gave neither me nor them any rest and drove

---

* (German) Dance of death.

us relentlessly on with the swashing bloodstream. I called my new friend Null (he was round, like all his comrades), and as our travels became more and more effortful and agitational, my warm feelings of friendship for this humble blood worker, who allowed me to bestride his toil-worn flanks, grew and deepened. The ferment I had incited in the veins of my Goliath was proliferating with astonishing speed: no doubt I had succeeded in jacking up the enemy's temperature.

Rather than count on the isolated protests of red blood cells that had joined me and Null, I instructed my friend to continue agitating inside veins while I infiltrated the enemy's lymphatic system. There my work proceeded more slowly and with greater difficulty: the sleepily flowing lymph impeded my progress and hampered communications, while the flaccid white blood cells inhabiting the milky mucous of that dull and sluggish little world were slow to adopt our battle slogans.

However, by dint of ceaseless effort, I did, on reaching the spleen, where white-cell youth grow to maturity, succeed in stirring up the ones whose membranes had not yet thickened and loosened. As a result, whole slews of draft-age white blood cells refused to go to the microbe front, while hordes of spirochetes, bacilli, rod-shaped predators, and poisonous spirilla invaded the organism's dermal borders.

Null, too, was wasting no time: when I returned from the lymph to the blood, it scalded me like boiling water. Everything was in an uproar. Revolutionary brigades of red blood cells were advancing on narrow capillaries where it would be easier to put up a fight. Some microbes had gone over to the side of those defending the old twenty-four-hour workday. The moment was approaching when (as we would say in our language) blood would be spilled, if it weren't already spilling continuously from arteries into veins and back again.

The thundering heart prevented us from massing our forces; it scattered our serried ranks with the cannonade of its pulse. I gave the order to retreat deep into the capillaries. But the furious blood pursued us even there: with salvo after salvo, it tore our forces from the vessels' slippery walls and hurled them back into the bloodstream. Then I gave the signal: *Build barricades!*

At first the work did not go well. But gradually, by patching together lumps of mucus, clots, clods of intercellular tissue, and the corpses of fallen fighters, we succeeded in creating vascular blockages.

But the joy of victory was short-lived. Gliding along on my faithful Null from barricade to barricade, I noticed that my mount was moving more and more slowly.

"Faster!" I cried, whipped up by the fever of battle. "We have to hurry."

Flapping his puffy sides for all he was worth, Null quickened his pace. Though not for long. The blood through which we were paddling had lost its fluidity: thicker and more viscous every second, it made any movement laborious and slow. Meanwhile a strange chill was creeping through the arteries' round pipes, causing their now glassy walls to contract.

Along the way, here and there, I saw groups of victors. Feebly milling around in the ever-thickening bloody mire, they stretched out their whitened ribs to me for answers and for help. Suddenly my Null fell over on his right side, squashing my foot. He tried to get up and couldn't. When I had finally wrested my hurt foot free, I tried to lift my fallen friend, but too late: he was dying. And while I fumbled with trembling fingers for the particular touch that in their language meant "Forgive me," death did its work. I rushed toward the fighters still moving:

"Retreat! Strike the barricades! Now! Follow me!"

But I too, with my limp, kept bogging down in the bloody sludge and could scarcely force my body forward. As for those legless blood cells, deprived of blood, they could not move. The thought slashed through my brain: *all wrong.*

So caught up was I in the fight against a man I hated, in organizing his death, it never occurred to me that when my enemy perished so would all my trusting and selflessly devoted friends. Oh, now the death of little red Null meant far more to me than did the demise of my colossal rival: I would have given the abductor of my love his life back in exchange for the life of my companion and comrade-in-arms, dear honest Null. Inside the squeezing and slowly collapsing arterial walls lay millions like him, killed by the will of my caprice.

The blood around me had long since stopped, but the blood flowing inside me had never rushed so profusely to my face: I felt ashamed to the point of nausea and disgust, ashamed of my ridiculous love and disgraceful rage. Was this why my teacher had entrusted me with the power of the blue tincture? That it might abet my pathetic passions and egotism?

Stumbling at every step over the corpses of my victims, deceived and killed by me, I began to search for an egress from the body of the giant whom I had likewise turned into a corpse.

I had to hurry so as to get out before the burial of that enormous mass of cold flesh. At first, though I was limping badly, my knowledge of anatomy helped me to find the right pathway inside the catacombs of the circulatory system. But then I took a wrong turn and was soon lost in a maze of small arteries. Meanwhile time was running short. Mustering my failing strength, I waded round and round, knee-deep in ichor and making almost no headway. A day went by like that. Another day was nearly over. The smell of decay, faint at first, was fast becoming a stench so vile I was close to losing consciousness. But the labyrinth of blood vessels, whose vaults sagged lower and lower, would not let me out. The thought that I would have to share the fate of my victims was assuming greater and greater probability. It's easy for philosophers, their noses buried in books, to dash off something about their contempt for death; but I would like to rub their noses in death's fetid torpor, in the tangles of limp rotting fibers and cells under which I staggered—then those transcendental fools would finally shake out of their books, along with the dust and cobwebs, all their digressions on death and immortality.

But no matter how my horror of the end spurred me, no matter how I strained my will and muscles, I soon realized that I could not outrun the funeral rites which, most likely, had already begun. Yet I did manage with what strength I had left, hacking through tissue oozing cadaverous poison, to reach the floor of a broad passage-way. Then my mind began to fog and I fell into nothingness. I don't know how long my swoon lasted: I suppose no more than an hour. When I revived, I saw a light glimmering faintly in the distance. And strangely: the cadaverous tissues under me were stirring. I didn't yet have the strength to get up. I merely ran my palm around me: the soft thick stems on whose matted tops I lay were rhythmically swaying, as if blown by a wind whose breath I could not feel, first ever so slowly backward, away from the light, then quickly and pre-cipitously forward, toward the light: away from the light—toward it;

away—toward; with every thrust my weightless body, gliding from stems to stems, drew nearer and nearer the glimmers of light. Without a doubt, I was on the esophagus's ciliated hairs, which retain the ability to move even after the organism's death.

Soon I was back on my feet and able to proceed, unaided by the ciliated stems, toward the tremulous light poking through the corpse's teeth into the oral cavity and even slightly farther. On reaching that dead orifice, I clearly heard the resonant strains of a requiem threatening to become my own. Working my soles for all they were worth, I fetched up at the broken filling just as voices beyond the gash-like mouth yawning overhead were singing of the last kiss.[32] I was forced to wait, though my predicament admitted of no delay.

When at last I scrambled out onto the surface of the corpse, I ran as fast as I could toward a side panel of the coffin, in a race to reach its edge before the lid did. I had gotten to the end of the dead man's shoulder and was already clambering onto the panel's flat rim when a stentorian creak from the wooden lid being lowered onto the coffin sent me dashing to and fro—its black shadow was looming over me, and I had to choose: either back under the lid, or onward at the risk of a crushing blow. I have always chosen and choose still: *onward*. Hurling myself athwart the panel's rim, I ran with eyes shut, every instant expecting to be flattened. With a dull shudder, wood thumped wood and . . . I opened my eyes and saw that the jaws of the coffin, clad in dark blue, had shut a half-step behind me, while I, having lost my balance, had fallen off the ledge and tumbled away, checked only by a tangle of silver strands, a glittering fringe that hung down to the ground. I instinctively grabbed one of those silver ropes and began to swing on it, feeling that I was saved. But then, trying to find a more comfortable position, I pressed my head to the whorled silver and noticed that my hair was just its color.

Yes, my friend, I escaped the wooden jaws that swallowed my enemy. But my youth was placed in a hearse that day, taken away and interred together with the millions of corpses buried in his corpse . . .

I shan't describe to you how, in a pile of black-bordered envelopes, I found the one with the name of the woman whom, such a short while ago, I had sought out and wanted. Now that name, whose very script had once made my heart beat faster, was forever cut off from me by the black lines that framed it.

I walked calmly inside the unsealed envelope and didn't even bother to spend time or strength on reading the death announce- ment, which soon spirited me—over a distance of hundreds of versts—back: to the phial. Or rather, phials, because the thought of that third glass post-horse, awaiting me in my teacher's laboratory, had gripped me with unexpected force. Sitting amid the envelope's four corners, I realized that that inscrutable tale of two pasteboard hearts had finally showed me its cards, while my confused musings on Aristotle's large and small man had come untangled: I, a micro- man, had known a macroman to the end: we had touched—not skin to skin, but blood to blood. And what all that spilt crimson blood had taken from me, I reasoned, the crimson drops in the third phial, when imbibed, would give me back.

On arriving at my destination, I made my way without incident to the glass symbol, and again it transformed me into *me*. In the apartment there wasn't a soul. I surveyed the familiar boudoir. The same perfumed disorder. In its old place lay her locket watch on whose dial my existence had so nearly ended. Turning up my sleeve, I could still see the deep scar left by its second hand. The scar had expanded with me into a long laceration now cicatrized. I picked up the watch; the hands were not moving: she had forgotten to wind it. I gave the little gold knob a few turns, and from inside came the ticking of time. I recalled the stingers of its bacilli: let them live— I am not vindictive.

Sprawled on the gold embroidery of my favorite sofa cushion was a man's collar, rather dirty. I peeked: size 16. I wear 15½. Well, what of it? Without a backward glance, I made for the door. But the door, as if anticipating me, sprang open: in the doorway stood she, still the same and yet *nothing* to me, the ovals of her slightly near-sighted eyes squinting in amazement. Behind her stood a tall, broad-shouldered youth shuffling shy feet, his face expressing a submissive joy: at the wave of her hand, he slipped into the next room, while she took two or three tentative steps toward me:

"You? But the door was locked: how did you get in?"

"Very easily: the postman dropped me in your mailbox yesterday."

"How strange: you're so changed."

"How ordinary: you're so unfaithful."

Her face turned a bit paler.

"I waited. I would have waited longer. But . . ."

"Your But is waiting for you in the next room. Though one day you'll step on his heart too. Good-bye."

I went to the door. Her voice detained me a minute more.

"Wait. Please: you must understand . . . As a person . . ." Her words trailed off.

"And are you sure that I'm a person? Perhaps I'm just a . . . stravaging Strange."

We parted. I hurried down the stairs and, without even stopping by my room, went off to see my teacher. Street clatter and din came at me from every side. It must have been a holiday: cheerful and unhurried crowds hung about on the sidewalks and at newspaper stands. But I walked on, eyes down. When I happened to look up, I saw a jostling bunch of yellow, blue, and red balloons, like enormous round drops, skimming through the air above the crowds. I quickened my pace. In less than half an hour, I . . .

■ □ ■

The storyteller fell suddenly silent.

"Teacher, I'm listening," I said. "In less than half an hour, you . . ."

He laughed:

"In less than half an hour . . . your train will leave. Quite possibly without you. Look at the clock: five past nine. It's time you went. Good-bye, my son!"

A minute later our eyes met for the last time: over the threshold. Then the door wedged shut, and the secret of the red tincture was left behind—as a key clicked loudly in the lock.

1924

CATASTROPHE

A multitudinous multitude of unnecessary and unrelated things—stones, nails, coffins, souls, thoughts, tables, books—dumped by someone for some reason in the same place: the world. Each thing is allotted a little space and a bit of time: so many inches in so many instants. All so-and-sos, great and small, whirl resignedly along their respective ruts and orbits. But if, say, star α in the constellation Centaurus should want to whirl, just a little, just once, along another star's orbit, then it must either rearrange everything in space (from brightest star to grayest dust mote) or allow chaos (only waiting for the chance) to overturn, tear up, and scatter the entire complex and cunning construction of orbits and epicycles. Whether the thinking of the old Sage,[1] of whom this story tells, ever once pursued the foregoing conditional disjunctive syllogism, I don't know. Yet I know for a fact that the Sage's thinking did nothing but go from thing to thing, searching out and extracting from those things their *meanings*. It then carried all those meanings, unrelated and unnecessary to each other, to the same place: the Sage's brain.

His thinking dealt with things, whether great or small, as follows: forcing apart their tightly conjoined surfaces and edges, his thinking tried to fathom the depths, and again the depths, to reach the thing's interior, wherein lay, in a single copy, *the thing's meaning*, its essence. After that, the edges and surfaces were, as a rule, put back in place—as if nothing had happened.

Naturally, there is no thing, however small or perishable, that does not find its own inimitable meaning inexpressibly dear and more necessary than necessity: with their rays, their thorns, their gimlet edges, their very smallness and perishability, things elude cognition, they defend their tiny "i's" from other "I's."

Always be compassionate toward the cognizable, my Wunder-kinder. Respect the inviolability of *the meaning that is not yours*. Before apprehending a phenomenon, think how you would like it if your essence were extracted from you and given to some other, strange, and hostile brain. Children, do not touch phenomena: let them live, let them appear to us as they appeared long ago to our fathers and forefathers.

But the Sage's thinking had no compassion. Catastrophe was inevitable. At first everything spatially close to the philosopher's head, everything "understandable in and of itself," was outside the circle of danger. The tops of the poplars rustling above the sleepy waters of the Pregel.[2] The church spires. The simpleminded people. The objects fixed firmly in space. The events reckoned by the church calendar.

The philosopher's thinking began to think from far away, glim-mering somewhere amid the glimmers of distant stars, in his *Theorie des Himmels**:[3] the Sage rummaged in a heap of white Dog Star rays, calmly and purposefully, as if this were not the sky, but the linen

---

* (German) Theory of the Heavens.

drawer in his father's antique bureau. How the stars reacted to this, if react they did, remains obscure. In the internal order of the constellations, certainly, no changes occurred. The souls of the stars are righteous, hence their orbits are rightful. The most meticulous astronomical calculations cannot show whether the stars glimmered *differently* after Kant than before Kant.[*]

Meanwhile an ominous rumor began to creep from thing to thing: the Sage, supposedly finished with the stars, was returning here, to Earth. Itinerary: the starry heavens above us—the moral law within us.[4]

Events went as follows: slowly shaking the stardust from its black feathers, the three-winged Syllogism,[5] contracting and collapsing the spiral of its arduous flight, drew nearer to these things.[6] And when those specks of stardust touched the gray dust of blind alleys and side streets, ripples of alarm and fearful horror ran through all earthly things. The orbits had been dealt with. Now it was the turn of streets—cart tracks—footpaths.

That is when catastrophe struck. Already frightened by Plato[7] and Berkeley,[8] phenomena, which in any case didn't really know whether or not they existed, did not of course wait for Reason with all its tools of inquiry: double hook-shaped §§s, clamps of exact definitions, and strings of paired antinomies.[9]

Space and time—throughout most of their earthly beachhead—became engulfed in panic. The first to try to jump out of their own limits were certain limited souls: they even created a special literary movement,[10] prompting a mass flight from the world.

---

[*] Author's note: In the late eighteenth century we still had sages, but no exact photometric instruments. Now we have the most sensitive instruments to measure the brightness of stars, but no sages. So it always goes.

Historians have been hard put to understand the gradual evolution of that panic. Here it is at its crest.

Churches taking to their heels, catching at the tiled roofs of little philistine houses, overturning those houses, overturning themselves, plunging their spires into the silt of sloshing lakes. Away raced centipedes—elephants—infusorians—giraffes—spiders. People trapped by the catastrophe in houses ripped from foundations went out of their minds, then dashed back into their minds, grabbed some useless quotation, the upside-down words of a prayer (such was their panic), and again went hurriedly out of their minds, senselessly whirling along their "I's"—now backward, now forward.

A detail: a bookcase from the Sage's apartment, having lost one stout carved foot, hobbled away on three feet and kept dropping this or that book with all its rustling pages in the mud. Inside the books, too, there was havoc: letters, syllables, and words rushed pell-mell along the lines, forming absurd (if now and then impossibly wise) phrases and aphorisms in unimaginable languages.

They say that an entire library suddenly crashed down from its shelves, crushing under piles of folio volumes the heart of a famous Romantic poet—and that heart, still rapping out a pulse, burst right out of his chest. Divided souls; smashed crockery; spilt soup (just then being brought to the Sage in a tureen, at the usual hour, from an eating house), drops of which quickly clung to grains of sand as the soup seeped (before it was too late) deeper into the earth. And the earth? The earth "rolled away like a little a-a-pple"[11] (la-mi-mi), cannoning into planets, bouncing over hollows along the star-cobbled way. The spires of cathedrals, peaks of mountains, needles of obelisks, and lightning rods rained down like the needles of pines in a high wind. Shards and potsherds, broken off in the cosmic chaos from their things, caught with their jagged edges at whatever they could: bizarre portmanteau things cropped up for moments and in moments fell apart (the moments, to save themselves, threw out everything unnecessary)—human tears on nimble spider legs, hearts stuck to the eyepieces of telescopes, etc., etc.

Chaos feels cramped in the narrow split of my pen.

Yet chaos has inserted itself.

In their haste, certain muddleheaded people even mixed up their "I's." (This is especially easy to do where psyches congregate—in families, sects, and so on.) Some minds, taking cover behind their reason, exposed that reason by thrusting it at the facts. Dispassionate Reason, ever true to itself, treated those facts as it did ideals and began to think of ideals as if they were facts. At one point, God and the soul fell into someone's hands, becoming palpable and visible, while a half-drunk cup of coffee ("*mehr weiss*"*) seemed an unattainable ideal. Discussion and intuition traded places. In some minds, eternity vanished into a crack; in others, the category of causality disappeared.

Morning glories, furiously twining their emerald spirals (at a speed of up to 186,000 mi/sec.), tried to unhitch themselves from a world gone mad.

The swash of panic, expanding and spattering incalculable icy drops, soon splashed as far as the stars.

Ecliptics[12] began to roll and pitch.

Twisting their rays into a blinding tangle, leaping out of their habitual orbits, colliding, igniting blue and emerald cosmic fires, the stars slid down orbitlessness out of *Raum und Zeit*.†

---

* (German) More white: *Milchkaffee*, or coffee with milk.

† (German) Space and time.

The parabolas of comets, which, as we know, have led since ancient times from spaces to infinity, began to resemble public roads during a procession of defeated armies.

Suns and planets, littered with the spangles of asteroids and meteorites, would throng a comet's path, hoping to be strung on the streak of its orbit: dropping whole human races—religions, philosophies, and all—into the void, they would stretch like a long blue-and-white necklace along the parabola's windings. Clouds of stardust glittered overhead.

And when everything had stopped shining, when everything, to the last apprehensive atom, had stopped making noise and settled down, there remained the old Sage, pure space (empty of things), pure time (empty of events), and several old books bound in vellum and embossed leather.

The books were not afraid that someone at some point might read them straight through to their meaning.

It remained to the Sage to describe pure space and pure time, now eerily empty, as if someone had overturned them and painstakingly scraped and shaken out of them every last thing and event. Describe them he did.

The folio volumes waited. The Sage slowly reached for them with the long cold fingers of a bony hand. A game began: the folios hid their mysteries among their faded, stuck-together pages. They rustled about this—and thought about that. The meaning of the text's letters tried to distract the Sage with typographical stars, to lure him away into broken lines of nonpareil and brevier; it hid among provisos and digressions, ducked behind parables and allegories.

In vain. The Sage patiently and graciously fitted keys to the codes. Discovering the meaning, page after page, door after door, he strolled through the whole enfilade of sections and chapters and came out the other side of the book.

In the meantime (if time it was), in émigré circles there reigned an unconcealed despondency.

"Accursed orbitlessness! Where exactly are we going?" snapped the bookcase we met earlier.

It had lost all its books and a second foot—and could barely drag itself along on the remaining two.

"To nothingness," mumbled the soul of a university lecturer from Jena.[13]

"The world is not to be."

"The world is not to be," rustled the last surviving pages of a *Manual of Logic*.

An emergency meeting was called by all the clockwork mechanisms.

For them a terrible *timelessness* was at hand.

On the one hand, according to the tick-tock talk of an antique chiming clock, all timepieces, due to the absence of time, would have to stop.

But, on the other hand, as a brilliant Geneva chronometer explained in precise philosophical terms and arguments based on authoritative sources, "Time, not being a thing, takes no material part in things."* Clockwork mechanisms are things. Ergo, once time is abolished, nothing in our clockwork gears, cogs, and mainsprings may change in any way—and those timepieces that have not run down before the moment when time is abolished, whose mainsprings remain wound,

---

* Author's note: This idea, in roughly the same terms, was defended later on (when order had been restored) by Arthur Schopenhauer (*Parerga und Paralipomena*, 2:13).

may *continue* revolving their hands (hour, minute, second), *as if nothing had happened.*

Accusations of backwardness and conservatism rained down.

The chronometer asked for a greater precision of terms: "So as not to fall behind the looming catastrophe, you propose that we all stop."

The matter was turned over this way and that, that way and this.

A majority of the wall and tower clocks sided with the gentle-voiced chimes. But the pocket watches and locket watches, which had all crept out of their vests and bodices,* voted with the chronometer. An unimaginable ticking rose up, an hysterical gnashing of alarm clocks. Spiteful pendulums swung into action.

Then suddenly came news that at first threatened to stop the creep of all hands and pinions, but then restored to seconds and inches all their rights to time and space: the Sage had died. This happened on the 12th of February 1804 at four o'clock in the afternoon.†

Some things, on hearing what had happened, did not wait for confirmations or elucidations but ran as fast as they could back to their instants and edges: once inside their *own* dear edges, they could not stop rejoicing that they were they. Legend has it that fastest of all was the soul of that university lecturer from Jena. Fair enough: a department chair had fallen vacant.

Other things, in their fright, were more prudent.

"Beg pardon," they said, "but who brought this news, how, and whence? In pure space, after all, there remained nothing except

---

* Author's note: No wonder the Sage had branded them with a contemptuous aphorism.
† Author's note: The centenary of this happy event was celebrated in 1904 by all universities and scientific societies.

a couple of books and the Sage's 'I' . . . It's a provocation. Fellow things, abstain from time and space. Patience."

However, everything was soon revealed and explained to the satisfaction of all concerned.

What had happened was this: the Sage, having described the "forms of sensibility," having cracked the code of the book that died for its right to be unintelligible—in short, having freed his "I" from dreams and words—asked, "Am I real?"

The philosopher's "I" had a great deal of experience: it knew the fate that always befell *the thing questioned after that question.*

No sooner had that "?" grazed his "I" than his "I" leapt out of quotes and, to put it baldly, took to its heels.

That is when the Sage's death occurred.

Little by little, events and things returned to their runnels—orbits—limits.

They say that the first to recover themselves were the souls of limited people. The rest came straggling after.

Now, as you may easily ascertain by touching your fingers to your face or to the pages of this book, everything is once again firmly and felicitously in its place.

Now, of course, we can even joke about it. But there was a moment when to frightened minds it seemed that all of this—the parti-colored and enormous (at first glance) spherical Earth flattened at the poles and the tiny, spherical, crystalline lens of a human eye—was one and the same.

Time slowly raised the heavy lids of the eye that had sought to perceive perception itself. That perception was strange and terrifying, but did not last long. The glassy eye has again been covered with a dead lid. Now, thank God, Earth and eye are separate. Now that the

Sage has done thinking and turned to dust, we are out of danger: there will be no more sages. As for the book left behind by the man turned to dust, I repeat: there is almost no danger for us, because it is easier to leaf through geological strata than to lift the pages, heavy with meanings, of the book of the Sage.

1919–1922

MATERIAL FOR A LIFE OF GORGIS KATAFALAKI

Even wrapping paper, freed of the object entrusted to its decorous gray nap, will not immediately cede the shape lingering in its folds and creases. True, the wrapping paper's resistance is easily broken once one has smoothed out its former corners and so proved to it, to the paper, that it is merely a shape-shifter, a plane vainly masquerading as volume.

From this, however, one should not infer that the writing paper awaiting a Life of Gorgis Katafalaki has special advantages over wrappings; it too can only catch the hazy shape of a many-sided human life. The meaning of the blackest ink is hopelessly gray as compared with the kaleidoscopic carousel of colors whirled about by existence.

What remains of the remarkable and instructive life of Gorgis Katafalaki? A smattering of facts; a dozen encounters scattered through a dozen middling memories. One need only, with one careless move, break the thread—and those days, round as pearls, will spurt apart, skittering away into cracks and dark corners. To recover any one of them, the biographer (his lot is hard) must bend down and scrabble in the darkness with his pen.

1

Perusers of the news in brief may recall—squeezed into three lines of nonpareil—the death of old Katafalaki. As he was stepping over some tram tracks, the elderly Katafalaki noticed an unaccountable red glint flashing in the distance above a boulevard turnstile. Intrigued by this phenomenon, Katafalaki stopped between the two steel parallels, fumbled his spectacles out of their case, hooked a wire earpiece behind one ear, and trained the lenses on the grimacing smudge; he managed to read—BEWA . . . and was flattened. Death's black bookmark blotted out . . . RE TRAM.

By way of inheritance, his son received only the empty wire rims from the spectacles, smashed by the blow of a cobble, and a pair of purely Katafalakian—extending like question marks from the bridge of his nose—ink-black eyebrows.

2

From a young age, Gorgis gave himself up entirely—from top to toe—to his passion for investigation, excavation, and exploration. All possible problems tugged at his brows and played on the furrows, as on an accordion. The ancients taught: philosophy begins in wonder.[1] There was no such thing at which Katafalaki could wonder enough: yet no philosophy came of it. This did not at all discourage Gorgis. Compared to Heine's melancholy youth[2] waiting by the sea for answers, exuberant Katafalaki had an enormous advantage: he always plunged—after his questions—into the water, unafraid of the waves or depths.

Learning did not come easily to him. His memory, like a torn drift net, never produced a catch. His whole life he confused Cervantes with Rosinante, Engels with Engelke, the transcendent with the transcendental, free verse with prose, and Kant with Conte.[3] No passages learned by rote, no rules of orthography, pounded like bungs into his brain by his teachers, would stick there. When his German tutor, who specialized in helping laggards, explained that *Mann* in the plural softened to *Männer*, Gorgis furrowed his brow and dug in his heels, insisting that man in the plural always hardened.

At any rate, without having mastered a single science, the young Katafalaki decided to formulate a discipline of his own. He did not aspire to great heights, nor did he claim that katafalakology should rank among the major, classified sciences. As a pioneer, constructing his framework at a remove, on the sidelines, he was so modest as to relinquish that natural right usually coveted by discoverers of even the most miserable grasses and pebbles: he renamed katafalakology haustology.

The story of this would-be science goes like this: while rummaging with his inquisitive pupils in the works of Ranke,[4] Katafalaki came across a footnote in which the German anatomist revealed his fascination with all manner of auricles. "The helix of the human ear is the most individual of all features to be found on the head of *Homo sapiens.* When in a crowd," the professor wrote, "I never allow my attention to wander, but concentrate on the auricles peeking out from under hats and hairstyles, noting the slant and design of the helixes, the formation of Darwin's tubercle,[5] the length of the lobe, and so on."

Other readers to whom this footnote was addressed most likely skipped over the fine print. But Katafalaki was a reader of a special sort—eyebrows working, he reread the note, again reread it, and decided: Ranke can have the ear, but his method . . . shall be mine.

The young trailblazer was in luck that day. A casual acquaintance, caught in the street by his sleeve, first nodded the brim of his hat on hearing of Ranke's auricles, then attempted to free his elbow, but feeling Katafalaki's fingers tighten their grip, ended by lending a dutiful ear to the drivel about ears. Suddenly the man's mouth began to stretch and twist—like a bicycle rim bent by an oncoming pole— into a figure eight. At once Katafalaki released his elbow. He had found his subject: *haustus*, the yawn. Up through the memory of a joyfully bemused Gorgis swirled the yawns that somehow always surrounded all of his (Gorgisian) aphorisms, stories, questions, and confessions: round, elliptical, parabola-shaped, suppressed, and crooked yawns fluttered about in his excited imagination. Wide vistas of classification, rivaling those of the German earologist, opened out before the founder of this new science: haustology. Yes, that worthy field of observation across which he, Katafalaki, would blaze as-yet-unbeaten paths. What could be more individual and more differentiated than the human yawn? The ear? But the ear can be severed even from a corpse, while only the living can yawn, and it is unseverable. Ears are static, and it's the rare person, Herr Ranke, who can wiggle theirs. That's right, whereas yawns . . . Granted, an earologist must overcome those difficulties associated with people's habit of pulling their hats down, but a haustologist has to catch yawns hidden behind palms, to hunt for them under pursed cracks of mouths, to trace the isotropy[6] of haustus in moist bulging eyes or driven inside quivering skin. And finally, a human being has no more than two ears, whereas his yawn is . . . Here the investigator's thinking ran into a knotty problem: the statistical tabulation of yawns. As he set about collecting yawns, Katafalaki exhibited persistence, patience, and sedulity: he hunted for haustus, gliding from lips to lips, as an entomologist does a rare butterfly flitting from flower to flower. Passengers on late-night trams rumbling down deserted streets did not notice through their half-closed eyes the observer with album open on his knees, sketching mouths distended by twenty-hour shifts. People shielding themselves with rows of beer bottles from the gypsy dances thundering onstage rarely turned their yawn-rent mouths toward the man they took for a worthless artist ready for a ruble to remind a man that he does have . . . a face. Frequenters of scientific gatherings, members of scholarly societies, associations, and academies where Katafalaki was conducted by his visiting card with its terse HAUSTOLOGIST in the right-hand corner, respectfully shook their colleague's hand and cleared a space for him near the water pitcher and the handbell rather than risk revealing gaps in their erudition with questions about the principles of haustology. Yet the behavior of this exponent of that rare science did strike some as a bit strange: he listened with his back to the speaker while scanning the faces in the audience; and if anyone covered their eyes with their palm, swayed in their seat, or hid their mouth behind a half-page of abstracts, he would fix them with his gaze, while his right hand tugged at the ties of his workbook with a movement recalling that of a hunter cocking his gun.

Soon—from gathering to gathering, from abstract to abstract, from problem to inquiry—the pages of this workbook began to fill with series of strange sketches recalling the lines of an nth order. This gradually accumulating material allowed Katafalaki to make his first attempts at a classification of yawns: zero-shaped, phytoid, parabolical, hooplike, funnel-form, drainpipe-type; yawns recalling an unbuttoned cuff or the Earth's orbit with elongated radius vectors; washbowl-type yawns; half-moon yawns; yawns in the shape of a garter pulled over one's knee, of a collection-box slot, of the *f*-shaped sound holes in a violin; yawns in the shape of . . . But one cannot list them all.

Katafalaki's sedulous pencil, ever in pursuit of the mouth-altering yawn, dogged its trail, stopping at nothing. The crudely gaping jaws of a night watchman, the polite crack of a consumer of abstracts, or the bared-teeth yawn of a prostitute still waiting for takers—these no longer interested him. Instead, he wangled his way into a session of the country's highest legislative body, where his black sketchbook captured something not included in the verbatim report. To friends Katafalaki graciously showed some of his rarest specimens: the yawn of a lover disenchanted with his mistress ("not so easy to catch," Gorgis's eyebrows twitched) and the toothless, ring-shaped yawn of an old crone at prayer, halfway through Our Father.

But then the hunt for splayed mouths ran up against an unexpected case that cooled Katafalaki's haustological ardor. During a summer trip in the south, he happened to observe the landing of mackerel. It was early evening, when the sea's blue sheen is shot with graphite. Strolling along the embankment, his black sketchbook under one elbow, the haustologist noticed, at the end of a perpendicular pier, a square of nets and boats. Near the moorings stood several wooden carts and a group of gapers. Katafalaki untied the ribbons of his sketchbook and made for the moorings. He arrived just as silver heaps of expiring fish were being loaded onto the carts. The thousands of mackerel layered up to the boats' oarlocks, their bodies coated with a blue-gray slime, seemed dead. But when a basket, drawn up from those piscan graveyards, was turned over, its silvery load raining down on the boards of a cart, the dead fish for the last time—for just a second or two—desperately twisting their scales, jerked and fought back to life, and their mouths, under white-sheathed eyes, stretched into square dead yawns strangely reminiscent of the half-open lips on tragic masks; but now fresh heaps of gasping mackerel were tumbling down on top of their splayed translucent mouths—more and more. Katafalaki reached for his pencil, but it too jerked in his fingers and froze. The ribbons of the black sketchbook were never again untied, while the science of haustology, for all its brilliant classificatory prospects, was never proclaimed. Katafalaki loved life too much; he might raise his eyebrows, but he could not knit them; the supply of smiles jostling in line for his lips was far from exhausted, while his rose-colored glasses, though they might fall off his nose, never broke. It would be absurd to demand that a sunflower become a moonflower and turn toward the stolen, blue-painted light of that nocturnal luminary. In short, the zigzag course of haustology would never take Katafalaki where his healthy heart—at seventy sanguine beats a minute—was urging him. Without a second thought, he abandoned the course.

3

Gentle Katafalaki, in recalling his various teachers, never resented them for having taught him almost nothing, though the *almost* they did manage to instill distressed him greatly. They were all too specialized: the finger obscuring a mountain seemed to them larger than the mountain, while eyes were needed only so as to wear blinders. After his portentous encounter with the heap of dead mackerel,

Katafalaki came to doubt even Ranke: his thinking had gotten stuck on Darwin's tubercle—and would not budge.

No, a polymath teacher with a broad, all-encompassing mind would not have led Gorgis Katafalaki into the windings of the auricle or the yawn's idiotic crack. There must be such an all-encompassing, universal intellect somewhere. They did exist: Aristotle—Descartes—Leibniz. He must find one. No matter what. So Katafalaki began his search. He surrounded himself with stacks of book catalogues, publishing prospectuses, bibliographical journals, and directories, hoping to run across the name he wanted. The surnames of scholars—agronomists, astronomers, botanists, balneologists, comedians, Dante scholars, dermatologists, demographers, Darwinists, Druidologists, gynecologists, geometricians, graphologists—harnessed to titles pulled loads from thousands of libraries along alphabets. But no matter how the letters rearranged themselves, the name of a great noncorpse did not emerge. Every unity was split along thousands of planes into thousands of pieces; every unit was fractured into fractions, and the swarms of minds that clung to each tried to fracture that fraction, so that some pens wound up with numerators, others with denominators. Katafalaki yawned, without even reaching for his sketchbook. He was ready to clap shut his bibliographical vade mecums and give himself up to despair when suddenly, in a German directory, he came across an odd combination of letters that recurred from page to page: Derselbe, derselbe, derselbe. It appeared in the Author column, but compared with other letter combinations (Müller—Schmidt—Jensen—Schneider—Linde—Klempe—Galbe), it demonstrated incomparably greater mobility and multiplicity. Where Lemke and

Galbe sat in this or that discipline, Derselbe's restless name wandered from science to science, undaunted by any logical or classificatory distances. Lemke wrote: "Cryptogams: Morphology and Taxonomy" (Jena, 1906); "On Cryptogams, Their Morphological Features and Place in Plant Taxonomy" (Jena, 1907); "The Cryptogamy of Ferns and Their Phylo- and Morphogenetic Characteristics" (Jena, 1908); "On Some Cases of Cryptogamy in the Fern Class" (Jena, 1909); "Again on Cryptogams" (Jena, 1910); "Some of My Disagreements with Professor Galbe on Dubious Cryptogamy and Pseudo-Sporulation" (Jena, 1911); "A Rare Case of Cryptogamy . . ." Whereas Derselbe wrote: "Spirals and Spirochetes" (Berlin, 1911); "A History of Philosophy from Ancient Times to the Present Day" (London, 1911); "Again on Transfinite Magnitudes" (Stuttgart, 1911); "Sixty-Six Ways to Hard-Boil an Egg" (Magdeburg, 1911); "The European Crisis" (Munich, 1911); "The Bantu Language Group" (Leipzig, 1911); "The Art of Being Coldblooded in Six Lessons" (Rome, 1911). Katafalaki was stunned: Derselbe's investigative range, his colossal erudition, scaling scholarly cliffs as if they were ordinary stairs, skipping over disciplines as if they were steps, caused the man in search of a teacher to thump the directory with his palm and exclaim: "Eureka!"

Now he had only to open the Encyclopedia to the letter D and find Derselbe's curriculum vitae: was he old or young, at which university was he a professor, and where should Katafalaki send his letter of request?

However, Derselbe was not in the Encyclopedia. The Lemkes and the Müllers and the Galbes and the Schmidts were all there, but Derselbe for some reason was not. Katafalaki grew pensive: what could be the meaning of this? An attempt at suppression? The intrigues of narrow specialists against a polymath? The envy of the Encyclopedia's compilers toward a genuine encyclopedist?

Katafalaki carefully reread his German directory. Strangely, the name Derselbe always came *after* the names of people writing on parallel or similar subjects: so not only the Encyclopedia, but even this directory was attempting to diminish, to conceal Derselbe's contributions. And surprisingly: the names of all those obtuse pedants and hairsplitters vying for first place were preceded by all sorts of honorifics—Dr., Prof., Acad., Inst. Memb. Derselbe's name alone stood unrecognized. What's more—Katafalaki gritted his teeth in indignation—here and there it wasn't even capitalized. So everyone was against the great, unsung Derselbe: even the typesetters. Now he understood why that repudiated genius had constantly to change cities: he was being persecuted, driven out, like all prophets who bring the world the truth, undeterred by stones or misprints. Katafalaki's eyebrows twitched with emotion as his lips mouthed the name of his teacher: that day he became a Derselbian.

Anyone else in Katafalaki's shoes would have turned from titles to texts. But that's just it: Katafalaki was in Katafalaki's shoes. He must write to his teacher straightaway: this thought popped into Katafalaki's head only a second before his pen dipped into the ink. With one ear bent over the paper, Gorgis gave his pen free rein:

Highly and Deeply Esteemed Doctor!
    Indian philosophers have called learning "a second birth." Hence I do most respectfully beg you to be so kind as to bring me to birth . . .

But here suddenly a second thought inserted itself: what am I doing? I should be writing to Dr. Derselbe in German. However, Katafalaki remembered no more than twenty or thirty German words. A dismaying obstacle. Armed with a German dictionary (the one he had used to decipher Derselbe's titles), Gorgis, sweat beading the furrows of his brow, began to hunt for the necessary vocabulary. His eyes might easily have come across the word that would have explained everything. But now a third thought, clapping the dictionary shut, prevented this: if Derselbe knew everything, said this thought, then he knew . . . Russian. With a sigh of relief, Katafalaki finished his letter and signed it with a flourish. He had only to address the envelope. But this proved not so simple: birds have nests, foxes have dens, but a son of man . . . Even the center of the world, if you believe mathematicians, is everywhere and nowhere— that is, it has no fixed address. The ink dried wordlessly on the tip of Katafalaki's pen, but his stubbornness was inexhaustible. Sitting lost in thought over lonely "Dr. Derselbe" marooned in the middle of the envelope, he suddenly smiled, again dipped his pen in the ink, added one more word above the name and, hiding his eyebrows under his hat, set off for the workshop of a sign painter. After that he had only to procure a passport and buy a ticket to Berlin. Katafalaki had more than enough patience, if considerably less money, but since his plan called mainly for patience, he hoped sooner or later to find Derselbe, without resorting to envelopes or people who, he suspected, would only try to thwart their meeting. Stanley, setting off for the wilds of Africa to find Livingstone,[7] did not know the languages of the local tribes. Gorgis Katafalaki was in the same position. His last doubt on this score was dispelled by an acquaintance, a very merry man (curiously, Katafalaki attracted only jolly types and jokers), who assured the departing Derselbian that if he knew just three words in every language—"please" and "how much"—he could easily and without any misunderstandings tour all of Europe.

A day later, as his train was pottering across Germany, Katafalaki reflected that he could have done with a fourth word: the station buffets greeted his hungry eyes every half hour with fan-shaped displays of sandwiches, but as he did not know the German for "sandwich," he reached Berlin on an empty stomach.

Nevertheless, once arrived in the Prussian capital, he gave himself up body and soul to the execution of his plan to seek out Dr. Derselbe.

Were he to turn for help to the authorities, to scholarly societies, to rivals, enviers, and ill-wishers of the great Derselbe (himself caught in the crossfire of their silence), he would be led astray, given false information and a wrong route. For news of Derselbe he could turn only to Derselbe and to no one else.

The plan devised by Katafalaki was both cunning and simple: pausing by the exit from the Friedrichstrasse Bahnhof, he opened his carpetbag and drew out a white banner lettered in red. He unfurled it, attached it to his walking stick, and slung it over his right shoulder; in his left hand he picked up his carpetbag and trudged off toward the city center, past the rising shutters of morning shops. First to notice the red sign (*Gut Morgen, Herr Derselbe!*) was a porter whose way was blocked by Katafalaki's flag. The porter's shoulders were bent under two hundred pounds, while the drops of sweat dangling from his eyelashes prevented him reading it through. The banner's letters landed next in the eyes of a chauffeur who had rolled up to the station steps; but then an address was called out, the motorcar's shiny side door clicked shut, and his hand gripped the gear lever as his eyes, together with the wheels, turned away.

Katafalaki, his *Gut Morgen, Herr Derselbe!* fluttering behind, strode down Friedrichstrasse, glancing now to the right, now to the left. His assumption was extremely simple: Dr. Derselbe, wherever he turned up, would, as a truly cultivated man, respond to the greeting addressed to him with at least a tip of his hat—and thereby identify himself. The Berliners in Katafalaki's path, accustomed as they were to sandwich men, paid no attention at first, but two blocks on, his banner set two fingers in motion: one finger—on the left side of the street—pointed at the moving letters, the other finger—on the right side of the street—beckoned to a policeman. As these gestures scarcely resembled greetings, Dr. Derselbe's seeker turned into Französische Strasse. Twenty or thirty rubbernecks followed after. Katafalaki heard laughter, then excited cries of protest, the first bars of a song he didn't know, a policeman's frightened whistle, and finally, someone's steady voice counting off steps. Turning toward the tramp of feet overtaking his flag, Katafalaki was amazed: unbeknownst to him, he had been cast in the role of standard-bearer, heading up a column of demonstrators. In his bewilderment, he dropped the flag and after a second's stupor barely managed to dodge the mechanical column's trampling tread. From the safety of a sidewalk, Katafalaki saw his hello to Derselbe, raised aloft by other hands, again fluttering above the marching ranks. It was plain as day: Derselbians, in hiding the world over, had risen against the system of suppression, had raised the flag of revolt, and were now on their way to overthrow all the old professorial chairs, pulpits, and authorities. Having regained his composure, Katafalaki dashed after his salutation swaying above the sea of heads: *Gut Morgen, Herr Derselbe!*

The procession, whose path the Spree tried to obstruct, spilled over one bridge, then another bridge, wound round the thousand-ton bronze statue of Kaiser Wilhelm, then the ribbed pile of the Berlin Palace, and made straight for the gold clockface of City Hall. The crowd, as if constricted, rose up on a thousand tiptoes, the letters in *Gut Morgen* inclined toward the ground: out onto the balcony of City Hall, bowing clockwise, came Dr. Derselbe. Katafalaki had imagined him somewhat differently: in reality, he was a man with a bald knobby pate and a smile superimposed on his round face, like a crescent moon on a half moon.

Speeches were made—Katafalaki understood not a word—and the peaceable crowd dispersed. Katafalaki alone remained with hat in hand, determined not to resume it until he had conveyed his feelings personally to Dr. Derselbe. Chance seemed about to grant him his wish: for out of City Hall's revolving door now emerged, surrounded by raised top hats, the great and incomparable Derselbe. Stopped by Katafalaki's low bows, he nodded genially, signaling his readiness to listen. One of his escorts knew Russian. Clasping hat to heart, Katafalaki asked in a joyful stutter if he indeed saw before him the author of tracts on finding the roots of imaginary numbers, on the art of extracting a viper's poisonous fangs, on the medicinal properties of ginseng root, on the chicken-and-egg principle in philosophy, and on sixty-six ways to hard-boil an egg. The small entourage looked surprised at the question, while the man to whom it was addressed eyed the beaming Katafalaki and turned on his heel. The rest followed suit, all except the translator, who hung back for a moment to explain to poor Katafalaki the following: the municipal council chairman's name was Lemke. Elections were held yesterday. The liberals nominated Galbe, while we conservatives stood behind the incumbent, three-term chairman Herr von Lemke. DERSELBE—*the same, the selfsame*—and no changes: that was our slogan. As expected, he won. Today—I don't know on whose initiative—the grateful electors came to greet their esteemed chief on the first morning of not his first and not his last, so we hope, term in office. It was—don't you think?—very touching . . .

The polite translator bent down to retrieve the hat that had slipped from Katafalaki's fingers, gave him an edifying nod, and hurried after the receding members of the magistrate.

Katafalaki stood rooted to the spot, as stock-still as the cast-iron spur stones lining Königstrasse. When at last he came out of his trance, he thought to put on his hat, but didn't dare: it seemed to him that there was *nothing* on which to put it.

4

Imagine a body which, pulled off its skeleton like clothing off a hanger, continues—through inertia—to shamble from spur stone to spur stone, flaccid, crumpling at the knees, with arms limp as empty sleeves: this was Katafalaki suffering the crisis and collapse of Derselbianism. Bending and unbending reflexes led his feet along Unter den Linden, but within him nothing worked, the thinking had stopped, like the mechanism of an unwound watch. Bending reflexes turned and took him past the white statues of Siegesallee. A ginger-haired sun shone overhead; in the merry blue air, children's green, yellow, and red balloons danced, tugging at their strings; gleaming bicycle rims, spinning nickel spokes, swerved in and out. Under the Tiergarten's animatedly gesticulating branches, rosy-faced Berliners strolled brightly about, pressing millions of steps into the springy asphalt. The luckless ex-Derselbian could not look up without seeing insultingly delighted smiles, eyes squinting against the sun, silver whorls of smoke from complacently puffing pipes. He cast about in vain, searching for a single glint to match the color of his mood. Even the shadows dropped on the ground by the bright emerald leaves seemed warm. Then suddenly Katafalaki's pupils froze: on a bench, wrapped in a black cape, shoulders slumped, sat a man. His face, half-obscured by his upturned collar, rested on the handle of his umbrella; beside him lay, sad and gray as its owner, a raincoat; shielded by the brim of his black hat from the brilliant sky, he was staring at the galoshes on his feet.

Katafalaki walked cautiously up. At the approaching shadow, the stranger quickly raised his head. Seeing only a man, he sighed and lowered it again. Gorgis sat down at the far end of the bench. Only the raincoat separated sorrow from sorrow. This emotional similarity plus the twenty German words at Katafalaki's disposal proved enough to ask a question, to receive an answer, and to understand it:

"*Morgen ist gut: warum ist kein 'gut Morgen'?*"*

Stranger:

"*Ich bin ein Meteorologe.* I am a meteorologist. And I predicted— predicted for today: clouds, heavy rain, heavy rain turning to hail. Or must I say that again?"

Katafalaki:

"*Bitte, noch einmal.*"†

---

* It's a good morning: why isn't it a "good morning"?
† Again, please.

The stranger, sullen as a storm cloud, made to roll up his raincoat, but on meeting Katafalaki's endearing smile full of genuine concern and commiseration, he softened and repeated very slowly:

"I am a me-te-o-rol..." His very first words elicited delighted nods from Katafalaki: I understand; then the rest somehow squeezed through. Gorgis gave the meteorologist's hand a reassuring pat and replied as best he could. The effort to understand him made the meteorologist frown:

"*Noch einmal.*"

Once again Katafalaki, with inexhaustible patience, set about rearranging his twenty words. In the dim glimmers of those two half-understandings, in Gorgis's dismal vocabulary, in the monotonous drizzle of one and the same sounds, there was evidently something that recalled bad weather, because the meteorologist brightened a bit.

Having exhausted his stock of German words, Katafalaki switched into Russian. And strangely, the affinity of feelings overcame the dis-affinity of languages. The conversation, painstakingly propped up with gesticulations on both sides, did not flag, but went on in this vein:

Katafalaki:

"Take heart—it looks like rain. *Es regnet.*"*

Meteorologist:

"Alas, that was just the spray from a passing water cart."

Katafalaki:

"Perhaps you'll say that those yellow dapples of sunlight came from a passing paint cart."

---

* It's raining.

Pause.

Katafalaki:

"Well, suppose it was: a water cart. Has it occurred to you that all these people walking past us, if they're smiling out of one corner of their mouth at the sunny dapples, they're smiling out of the other corner at you? That's right, I know what I'm saying: for a pastry to seem doubly delicious to a child, you must first promise him a whipping. Then go back on your promise and . . . You threatened to lash all these people with heavy rain, but gave them on a gigantic blue platter the sun they so love. All eyes are on you, and only on you, the organizer of this delightful surprise, but you don't even notice; you hide under the brim of your hat, as if . . ."

Katafalaki felt a lack even of Russian words. But his eloquence had already had its effect: the morose predictor of downpours wrested his chin from the handle of his umbrella and scrutinized the stream of passersby. The man in galoshes with his raincoat at the ready was indeed attracting attention and laughter.

"Well?" said Katafalaki.

The faint suggestion of a smile crinkled the meteorologist's lips. He shook Gorgis's hand. From that day they were fast friends.

5

Joachim Vitsling gave refuge in his observatory—amid the whirling weather vanes, series of thermometers, barometers, hygrometers, dust counters, gangly tubes measuring precipitation, frogs suffering in the name of science, wall diagrams, and countless other calculators—to Gorgis Katafalaki.

At first Gorgis only eyed the various instruments and the barograph curves predicting the circulation of cyclones and anticyclones, but then—under Vitsling's guidance—he was gradually drawn into the work. As a little boy, Gorgis had liked to fold back a few leaves of the tear-off calendar[8] to discover that (hurrah!) next Sunday for dessert there would be fruit compote—and any discordance between calendar leaf and cook distressed him almost to tears.

So it was now. In helping to compose the weather bulletins, Gorgis felt like the gambler who has bet on the horse Helios—now in a double, now in a single—while the wail of the alarm clock to begin the day was like the gunshot at the starting gate.

Katafalaki was out and about first thing, and not a man in all Berlin held his head higher: the meteorologist's pupil did not want to miss a single vicissitude in the contest between clouds and sun. If the day before he and Vitsling had bet on the sun, Katafalaki, somewhere in the middle of Küstriner Platz,[9] would smile encouragement at Helios's gold chariot bowling up from behind the pitched roofs or, shading his eyes with his palm, squint uneasily at the rain clouds like powder-gray apples, straining to descry behind their onerous hurry even one golden lash delivered by his "favorite." If the sun overtook the rain clouds and made for the zenith, Katafalaki would dash into a café and indulge in a coffee *mehr weiss,** feverishly crumpling his newspaper as he compared the weather bulletin with the growing blue gap between sun and rain-cloud croups. But it was still too soon to celebrate: the sun—around the last bend—might break stride, the rain clouds might pick up their pace, and then . . . Katafalaki would realize only come evening, when the race was over and the day at the

---

* More white: coffee with milk.

finish line, as Berlin bells tolled the Angelus,[10] that he had not had his midday meal. All in all, he had become entirely—from top to toe—absorbed in his new profession. "It was easy for Kant," he often said, "to operate with pure space, where you don't need galoshes, where it's not sunny, not cloudy, not wet, and not dry. But try and tinker, as Vitsling and I do, with our space, damn it, where it's fine one minute, foul the next." For his meteorological amusement, Katafalaki would give the wind marks, as if the wind were a schoolboy who hadn't learned to blow (low marks) or, on the contrary, had blown up a storm (top marks).

So they lived, Vitsling and Katafalaki: if they often quarreled with the weather, their own friendship was cloudless. Then one day Vitsling, having glanced at the bulletin, which clearly—in black and white—indicated "clear" skies, forgot to glance out the window. He went out in light shoes and no coat, hat in hand and face tilted up to the bulletin's sunshine, only to be pelted by a cold downpour mixed with hail. Pretending not to notice, Vitsling pursued his way, whistling merrily and fanning himself with his hat against the transcendent heat, until the icy rain began to beat down on his lungs and drum on his proud heart. That evening, in bed with a temperature of 104 and a beatific smile, the half-delirious meteorologist kept saying: "But I said it would be hot." Two days later Vitsling's body was at room temperature, and a day after that—at exactly the temperature of the ground in a Moabit graveyard.

Katafalaki was beside himself. Every street thermometer reminded him of his departed friend. Their strong mercurial stalks now rose up, now sank down, shedding degrees, while the green stalks of grass on his friend Joachim's grave grew only higher and higher. Berlin, which Katafalaki could not forgive for the loss of Derselbe and the death of Vitsling, became hateful to him. He must turn for help to a train station. Which one? It didn't matter. The day of his departure, the wind was driving rain clouds into the southwest. Katafalaki bought a ticket to Paris.

6

Having installed himself in a cheap family-run hotel on the Boulevard Saint-Michel, Gorgis Katafalaki decided at last to anchor himself to a profession. Life's blows had taught him humility. It's unclear what associations made him choose a school for tooth drawers; perhaps he wanted to settle old scores with haustus, to have a proper rummage with pliers inside cotton-stuffed yawns thrown back on the leather headrest of a dentist's chair. At any rate, this man attracted to the stars decided to become a man who extracted teeth.

At first all went well: Katafalaki could soon tell an eye tooth from a canine, an abscess from a fistula; he knew that wisdom teeth clung to the jaw with a single or a double root, complicating the work of his pliers; he learned to maneuver inside a fitfully jerking yawn with the buzzing needle of his drill and, finally—having gripped the brittle tooth in a steel vise and pinned the patient's jumping kneecaps to the chair—to weed bone from bone, as grass from the ground.

But an innate compassion for the agonies hidden under kerchief-bound ears set Gorgis's restless mind searching for ways to alleviate and abbreviate his patients' torment. If Heine said that "love is a toothache in the heart," then to Katafalaki the suffering that sent one to the dentist was an unhappy love affair in the tooth. A simple "Be patient, Monsieur" or a long dig with needle and pliers inside the painful cavity would not suffice: he must devise a heroic and head-long means of expunging the disease once for all.

The school's director, an elderly, lop-lipped Portuguese Jew, whose spectacles had peered into tens of thousands of yawns, who spoke to students and patients in a mishmash of eleven languages, was very surprised late one night when the bell shook him out of a sound sleep. Puzzled, he got up and, candle in hand, went to the door:

"Who's there?"

"Katafalaki."

The old dentist drew back the bolt—the student's raised eyebrows peeping round the door nearly bumped into the eyebrows, no less raised, of his teacher. Mumbling his excuses, Gorgis asked if he might have a few minutes. The teacher brought his candle closer: the eyes of his nighttime guest glittered with an ecstatic light; his wide, kind smile revealed two rows of strong white teeth; under one elbow, he had a small box. Still puzzled, the teacher gestured with his candle toward the study and asked his guest to be brief. Katafalaki gladly obliged: his discovery—like everything revolutionary, radical, subversive—fit easily into a dozen words. He clicked open his box: inside were five or six rows of tiny ampoules filled with a brown substance; from each ampoule dangled a thin wick.

"Enough of suffering!" Katafalaki exclaimed, stifling a nervous spasm in his throat. His index finger pointed to the long-tailed capsules.

"What have we here?" Candle and spectacles bent over the box.

"Dynamite."

The candle swayed and made for the door. But the inventor, now busily explaining, was too carried away to notice.

"It's very simple. Instead of all those dry and wet wads of cotton, you insert an ampoule in the cavity of the diseased tooth, light the fuse, and bang!—the tooth is reduced to dust."

"And what about . . . the head?" asked an irate voice from the hall.

A deathly pallor overspread the inventor's face:

"I hadn't thought of that."

The glissando of invective in eleven languages was capped by the slam of double doors. Next day the man who hadn't thought had to think of a new profession.

7

While still living in Berlin, Katafalaki had complained about the traffic: the city, like a torn sack, was always disgorging people, whirling wheels, jerking pedals, rollers running on wires, swaying springs and carriages, all of which got in his way: right turned into left, disorienting him and breaking the line of his route with colliding crossroads, driving him into perpendicular bystreets and muddling his steps. But those longtime Berliners who listened to Katafalaki's lamentations usually said that this was nothing, whereas in Paris, for example, one could easily become completely lost in the crowd.

Those words stuck in Katafalaki's mind. He had no intention of becoming lost. People like him did not grow on trees. Were he to lose himself, Gorgis Katafalaki, in the metropolitan maelstrom, where would you find another?

Yes, one couldn't be too careful. Which is why, when strolling about Paris, before crossing a crowded square or rushing thoroughfare—the Place de la Concorde, Rue de Rivoli, Boulevard des Italiens, Place de l'Étoile—Katafalaki would pin a visiting card to his left lapel, just in case. Having dodged between the madly lunging vehicles, his eyes darting in all directions, he would at last feel the opposite curb underfoot, glance down and read: GORGIS KATAFALAKI. With a smile of relief, he would unpin the card looking as if he had just received a brand-new Katafalaki out of a bandbox and need only remove the tag.

But one day something was pinned on Katafalaki together with the card, causing the life of our hero to take an exceedingly strange turn.

That day he had forgotten to unpin his card. It was a hot thundery afternoon, when people are either sleepy or irritable. Katafalaki, sitting in a café over a bottle of cider, felt sleepy; the two dandies in bright ties at the next table felt irritation. Through his cloudy cider and semi-somnolence, Katafalaki did not notice the little white square still fastened to his lapel, but the dandies (one named Mildiou, the other Louis Tuline), in search of a mark for their bilious mischief, did—and decided to play a joke. Tiptoeing up to the nodding stranger, Mildiou unfastened the card and replaced it with his own. For a minute the friends had fun reading and rereading the purloined surname: "Ka-ta-ha-ha-fa-hee-hee-la-ki-ho-ho!" Meanwhile the thundercloud hovering silently over the roofs, filling the air with shimmers of bile, seemed to prick up its huge dirty ears and wait: what next?

M. Mildiou, flipping the card about in his fingers, shifted his gaze to another table at which sat—over two glasses of orangeade, smiles entwined—a couple. M. Mildiou twirled his moustache and remarked, loudly and distinctly, to M. Tuline:

"If not for that flighty lady, one could die of the heat."

The thundercloud began, discreetly if merrily, to rumble. The suitor, insulted, scraped his chair aside and strode up to Mildiou. Roused by the commotion, Katafalaki opened his eyes just as the opponents were exchanging cards. Afraid of becoming a witness to a scuffle, he quickly paid and left. At twenty paces it began to pour. By the time he reached his room he was soaked. While hanging his sodden jacket on the bedpost, he noticed, stuck to the nap, a white blotch with smudged letters on it. But how strange: the name on the card had shrunk and mixed up the letters. In the room it was dusk. He snapped on the light and looked closer: those rain-blurred letters were definitely not his—and just as definitely six or seven were missing. Katafalaki even turned the card over, but saw no sign of the vanished letters. It was then that he first felt suspicious. For a minute he sat lost in thought. Then he peeked round the door. Not a soul. All the better. He crept down the passage—past a dozen closed doors—to a dark alcove where (he recalled) stood a mirror. The cheap glass in which no one had looked for ages had perhaps forgotten how to reflect: at least when Katafalaki, wry-mouthed from anxiety, bent over its surface gauzy with dust and cobwebs, the surface responded with only a fuzzy, crooked, greenish-gray shape, the shape of a man in general, one who didn't care if he were fat or thin, sexless or sexed, extant or only a revenant.

From the far end of the corridor came the sound of footsteps. The man who was so recently Katafalaki sprang away from the mirror and slipped back to his room. He had best not show his face for now and consider how to be without himself. That night he didn't sleep. Ex-Katafalaki now paced to and fro muttering

("No, this is the most inexcusable absentmindedness—to lose myself—like a needle in a haystack—damned Babylon—to drop myself, like a pocket handkerchief—what nonsense!"), now bent over the bleary letters and tried to guess his new name. His efforts were in vain: the smudges would not form a name. Come dawn, he dozed off. An abrupt knock at the door reopened his eyes. The man with no name turned the key. Two men in top hats, smiling politely, handed him a written challenge and asked him to name his seconds so they might settle on the time, place, and weapons. Someone else's life was beginning, a highly inconvenient life full of the unforeseen. Well, what of it? If in haste you grab someone else's galoshes or "I" and don't notice in time, it's utterly useless to complain that that new "I" is tight or that those strange galoshes keep falling off your feet. Hanging his head, the man who had lost himself in the crowd asked:

"Whom do you take me for?"

The courteous top hats replied:

"For Gorgis Katafalaki,"—and were somewhat taken aback when the future duelist, suddenly beaming, fell to vigorously shaking their hands:

"Aha! So I am Katafalaki, and not that thing of smudges! It's very kind of you to consider me Katafalaki, very noble, and what's more . . . You have given me my life back. That's right. I'm deeply touched."

Having shed his "ex," Katafalaki felt born again—they might fire at him, wound him, kill him, but they would fire at him, at Gorgis Katafalaki. He existed. He was that which could be hit, or even (ha-ha!) missed, and that was all that mattered. That day—possibly his last, yet in some sort his first—Gorgis Katafalaki, whistling merrily, wandered the streets, choosing, however, ones less crowded.

The meeting of two bullets had been set for five the next morning in the Bois de Meudon. A small flat-bottomed steamer, red paddles plunging into the Seine, took Katafalaki and his seconds to the Meudon landing stage. The dawn fog prevented them seeing farther than ten paces (incidentally, the distance for the opponents had been fixed at fifteen paces). They walked past a cluster of summer cottages, and soon mosses were crunching underfoot. Forest. Only now—amid the spectral shapes of trees swathed in fog, their branches outstretched like the arms of ghosts in photographs at the Society for Spiritualistic Research—only now did it occur to Katafalaki that he, in another ten or twenty paces, might stumble into his grave and never know: for what? He made up his mind to dispel at least one of the two fogs obscuring the meaning of these events. But nothing turned out as he had anticipated. Before he could say a word, his opponent, as they started walking toward each other, pointed at him and declared:

"That is not Katafalaki."

Now that hurt. If the man had said: that is not Dupont, that is not Garnier, not Couteau, not Patarre, not whoever—the misunderstanding would have gone right up in smoke, while the smoke from their pistols would have remained inside the muzzles in the form of pure possibility. But this attempt to rob him of his name—lost and then found with such difficulty—Katafalaki could not let that go unpunished:

"Repeat that."

"Certainly. You are not Katafalaki."

"And you are not a man, but a coward who takes his shot before the command: '*Marchez!*' Katafalaki may lose his way, yes, but lose his head—never! And we will fire at each other until I have forced you to admit that I am indeed Katafalaki. To the barrier!"

The seconds were thrown into confusion, while the suspected-of-nonexistence Gorgis went on shouting, demanding a duel. Now that he had his "for what," he was not about to renounce Schopenhauer's thirty-second and last eristic argument: bullets.[11]

In the end the pistols were loaded, the opponents took their positions by the barriers and cocked their guns. At the last moment Gorgis heard from a branch on high, above the fog sailing into the sun, the flutelike staccato of an oriole. As for what happened next, there are two versions: one says that the bullets, whistling like the oriole's song, flew peaceably asunder; according to the other, one of the bullets banged into Katafalaki's brow, rebounded aloft, and struck the little songbird, whose corpse, rustling down through the leaves, came to rest between the two barriers—and no more blood was shed due to the sudden appearance on the forest path of two fast-approaching figures: Guy Mildiou and, scarcely able to keep up with him, Louis Tuline.

What had brought them there requires no lengthy explanation. After the incident in the café, Guy waited the rest of the day for his seconds. In vain. The next day, in doubt as to the vengefulness of his opponent, he decided that the duel had been called off. That evening he was regaling his usual drinking companions with two tales—to be illustrated with two cards. One card (with the name and address of "the not fearless knight" who declined to meet "the not irreproachable knight,"[12] as Guy's friends laughingly dubbed the opponents) was passed around, but the other card was nowhere to be found. Mildiou ransacked every compartment of his wallet, then started on his memory and suddenly clapped himself on the forehead: in the café, in his excitement, he must have presented not his own card, but that of his dozing neighbor. His friends redoubled their merriment, but Mildiou felt abashed. He must clear this matter up at once. Having waited out the night, Guy and his inseparable Louis set off for the address on the card. They were not a hundred paces from their object when the entrance door flew open: three men walked out; a waiting motorcar rumbled to life; one of the three looked back. "There he is!" cried Guy and rushed ahead only to remember that dueling etiquette forbade combatants to speak to each other. He turned round and beckoned to the lagging Louis, meanwhile the motorcar drove off. The morning streets were still deserted. Only at a crossroad did the friends find a fiacre. Its cracking whip set off in pursuit of the car's shrieking siren. They overtook the motorcar only because it had stopped at a landing stage on the Seine. Jumping out of the fiacre, the friends heard a gangway rattling back and the hoot of a steamer casting off. They had no choice: they climbed into the now free motorcar and told the driver to follow along the riverbank after the steamer. That was not hard to do. But then the steamer, having paddled for some twenty minutes, tied up at the opposite bank. The nearest bridge was half a mile back. The motorcar circled round and was nearing the mooring when again the steamer hooted and chuffed off. Ten minutes later it was sidling up to the landing stage at Meudon, again on the opposite bank. This time there was no bridge: the friends flung themselves into a rowboat. It was less their inquiries than their intuition (the glades in the Bois de Meudon had long since been tamped down by duelists) that put Mildiou and Tuline on the right track. The curtain of fog rose on the final scene in this comedy of errors: in the wings either side, symmetrical groups of seconds; by the footlights, separated by fifteen paces, two muzzles pointing down; center stage, bright ties—Guy and Louis. If before, during the exchange of cards, a thundercloud had hung over their heads, then now, after an exchange of shots, in the interstices between the branches, a gold-flecked morning blazed blue. What's more, when the pistol barrels are empty, it only remains to fill the glasses. A little restaurant on the edge of the forest saluted with a dozen corks, and by noon the return steamer, with a merry hoot, had deposited eight passengers—carrying one small flat box with recessed catch between them—at a Paris pier.

8

The case of mistaken cards and brows brought Gorgis together with M. Mildiou and his sidekick. People who liked of an evening to visit the fairy lights on Montmartre were sure to see Katafalaki promenading between two bright ties. To Messrs. Guy and Louis— sedulous collectors of anecdotes, sanguine sorts who prepared the smile on their interlocutor's face like a complex and well-seasoned dish—Katafalaki was a rare and valuable find. It would take too long to list all the practical jokes they played on simple-hearted Gorgis. An example or two will do.

One day, as the three were roaming the dusty and busy Paris boulevards, Gorgis confessed that he would not be averse to spending next Sunday in some lovely hamlet, far from the din and stone. His Parisian friends exchanged winks—and promptly offered him this advice:

"Well then, go to Complet."

"Yes indeed, why not go to Complet?"

Katafalaki thanked them and wrote down the name.

Next morning, he began scanning the signs above the windshields of omnibuses and autobuses. Some proposed Clichy, others beckoned to Belle-Île, still others promised the airfield at Issy, or the paths of Charenton-le-Pont, Neuilly-sur-Seine, Saint-Cloud, Vincennes, and distant Fort d'Aubervilliers. But above the flicker of spokes, amidst the race of names, nowhere did he see a sign for Complet. Katafalaki had begun to doubt the existence of such a route when from around a corner, fat tires coming right at him, lumbered a long omnibus through whose dusty windshield glimmered: Complet*. Overjoyed, Gorgis ran as fast as he could toward the footboard of the sagging caravan and, before grabbing the handrail, cried out:

"Complet?"

"Complet!" came the reply. The door slapped shut, and the omnibus, spewing fumes in the face of a dumbstruck Katafalaki, rattled off around another corner. Katafalaki decided to wait for the next bus. Past him, pressing ribbed tires into the heat-softened asphalt and belching smoke, trundled autobus after autobus, omnibus after omnibus; again Vincennes, Issy, Charenton, Clichy, but, as if to spite him, no Complet. Finally there appeared a shiny black autobus full of laughing people in fancy dress. Sporting a large sign for Complet, the bus raced past without even pausing at the stop, while its passengers waved handkerchiefs and umbrellas at the inexplicable man who, for a good city block through a whirlwind of dust, raced after

---

* Full up.

them. But Katafalaki was not easily discouraged. Wiping his perspiring eyebrows, he stood at another crossroad, determined to do whatever it took to get to Complet. Again he saw a string of unwanted Vincennes and Charentons, and then a bus filled to capacity rumbling toward the longed-for Complet. Wavering between hope and despair, Gorgis felt the way you do in line at the box office a few minutes before the play is to begin. The clock hand moves strangely fast, the line strangely slowly; now the ushers are dashing about, the cloakroom counters deserted; a latecomer, mistaking coat check for ticket, asks where to go; the lobby lights dim and through the diamond-shaped cutouts in the house doors comes an excited hush; meanwhile the man blocking the ticket window counts his change; there's still time—the window is quickly coming nearer; the wall-muffled first bars of the overture—what a shame; but never mind, you could still make the curtain—between your money and a ticket there are only four backs; no—three, two, one—then suddenly the window bangs shut, while outside a dully drizzling rain, slick pavements, and dreary turns from street to street take you back the way you came.

The sun was already sinking when the exhausted Katafalaki, having watched the last crammed "omnibus to Complet" out of sight, abandoned his crossroad and plodded home, to his bleak and lonely room. "How marvelous that Complet must be," he mused, "if so many people want to go there. Chin up, my friend, a little patience, and tomorrow you too will be lolling in the Complet meadows."

Next morning, he was again at his post, and again dozens of four-wheeled conveyances, showering him with fumes and soot, whooshed past, again the doors to Complet slapped shut in his face and rude conductors pushed him off footboards, while the teasing sign "Complet" curtained itself, again and again, with smoke and dust. Chagrined and indignant, the would-be passenger returned at dusk to his room. He did not understand why everyone else could go to Complet, but he could not. He clenched his fists at the thought of all those bowlers and bonnets jamming the Complet line—they had delighted in its shady groves and lounged by its ringing fountains, while he had come back with nothing. His dreams that night were restless and fitful: a reverie proved more amenable than an autobus—easily and soundlessly it whisked him to the magical, achingly marvelous Complet: a fragrant, many-colored carpet of flowers underfoot; emerald branches swaying like fans overhead; a thousand-beaked song mingling with golden streaks of sunlight; a gentle wind dandling reflections of shores fallen into ponds and pools.

Shaken out of his visions by the morning knock at the door, Katafalaki fumbled feet into shoes and again set off for the bus stop. Only on the fourth or fifth day did a Paris acquaintance, winding his way amid the race of wheels, happen to catch sight of a gaunt, hunched, unshaven man in whom he hardly recognized Katafalaki:

"What are you doing here?" asked the acquaintance.

"I'm waiting for a bus to Complet," replied Katafalaki's shadow, raising sad sunken dark-ringed eyes.

The Frenchman first shrugged his baffled shoulders, and then, throwing his head back, roared with laughter. His laughter was promptly joined (such is a Paris street) by a dozen smiles—and soon the legend of the mysterious and unattainable Complet had become a humorous catchphrase. That day Gorgis Katafalaki increased his knowledge of French by one word.

But it would take too long to untangle the entire tangled clew of practical jokes invented—tailored to aspects of their new friend's nature—by the indefatigable Messrs. Guy and Louis. Suffice it to recall the final foolery, which cut short the clew, the friendship, and Katafalaki's sojourn in Paris.

M. Guy, you see, had long sought without success the hand of a charming young girl. That is, he had success with the girl, but not with her parents, patriarchal rentiers who insisted that until—as tradition demanded—they had married off their elder daughter, their younger (Guy's object) must have patience and wait. Guy and his love were in despair: where nature had lavished on her a delicate oval face, wide-set blue eyes, a gentle voice, and a shapely figure, it had skimped on her sister, whose face was truly unsightly. Guy, who had labored in vain to find suitors for this fright, decided that kindhearted Katafalaki would be the perfect match for his future *belle soeur.**

First he must prepare the ground. Indeed, the ground was already fairly mellow and yielding. To his arguments about the need to marry, Gorgis would nod: yes, yes! But whom? The arms of the problematic suitor hung like puzzled crosspieces in the air. The merry schemers exchanged winks and began extolling a charming blue-eyed creature who would not be averse to taking the name Katafalaki. Gorgis's eyebrows never arched so high as they did then. He smiled bemusedly, straightened the knot of his tie and asked: who *is* she?

The next day Guy introduced Gorgis to his bride. This pretty French girl, apprised of the scheme, captured Katafalaki's imagination with the first gaze of her half-closed eyes gleaming blue through

---

* Sister-in-law.

dark lashes; listening to her melodic nothings, to the oriolish tones of her flutelike voice, he would now and then clutch at his collar, trying to stop his head from spinning like a top. When she laughed, Katafalaki would squint and those pearly peals became a pearly rain of falling pearly teeth; on opening his eyes, he would see with a sigh of relief both pearly strings unbroken between her merrily purpling lips. The wine, which had done its work in four glasses, was a marvelous accelerant and, on the way home from the café, Gorgis, enchanted almost to tears, asked his lady (Louis and Guy were twenty paces behind): "Are you never afraid of being so beautiful?" and "Would you consent to be my wife?"

The French girl, hiding her smile under the shadow of her hat, said that she would consider it. Katafalaki asked for a rendezvous and it, after a decent pause, was granted: tomorrow, at seven in the evening, Parc Monceau, by the statue of Maupassant.

Next morning Katafalaki began to hurry time. First he drew a dial with the hands at seven o'clock, placed it beside the dial of his own ticking watch, and waited for them to become alike. Then he drew six hundred sticks symbolizing minutes, and after every circuit of the second hand gladly crossed off a stick. Twenty-five minutes past eight was, to his mind, six hundred and thirty-five minutes before seven. Incidentally, it was at exactly twenty-five minutes past eight that the business of crossing off sticks was interrupted by the sudden appearance of M. Louis. Gorgis was delighted: he seated his guest opposite him, took his hat and, clasping it excitedly to his breast, declared that today he was a happy man. M. Louis confided that today he too had a great joy and had come to share it with Gorgis, as someone who could be trusted with a secret. Katafalaki moved his chair closer still: he was all ears.

"Today," Louis began, "I completed my investigations into the tuning of the sense organs. That's right, our nerve fibers, like the strings of an instrument, can easily be regulated—I have proved this experimentally—with, well, let us say . . . pegs. You are no doubt surprised, dear M. Gorgis, that I, such an apparently frivolous man, could devote myself to scientific research. And yet it is so. Appearances deceive. While still at university, I stumbled on the idea of tuning nerves. My initial assumptions were simple: if a drum skin, depending on the tension, will produce, at the touch of a drumstick, different sounds, then our eardrum, pulled taut by chemical agents, will produce, at the touch of this or that drumst . . . I mean to say that stimulation of the eardrum with one and the same frequency will produce completely different sounds. Transposing these experiments from acoustics to optics, I soon achieved equally positive results. True, I struggled for three entire years with the design of my apparatus, but today I turned the last screw, and before long a statue of Louis Tuline will stand beside that of Pasteur."

"Why not of Maupassant? In the Parc Monceau?" Katafalaki smiled dreamily.

"Because I have discovered something greater than anti-plague serum. I have found a cure . . . for unhappy marriages. Unhappy marriages are far more widespread than the plague. You may soon become convinced of this yourself: through experience."

"I don't understand what this has to do with . . ."

"Everything. My apparatus for tuning eyes will be extremely cheap. No more costly than a tuning fork plus a key for piano pegs. In the course of a long marriage, you see, the pull of passion gradually weakens; habit dulls the perceptions of man and wife, they no longer see each other as they once did; the honey begins insensibly to sour—and that is perfectly natural: our eyes and ears do not stay in tune, they get out of tune and play off key, like a family piano incessantly pounded on with all ten fingers. If you don't mind paying five francs every few months to tune your piano, then you'll be only too glad, I hope, to part with another five francs to tune your marriage. That's right, this will all be extremely easy and convenient: if, say, a wife notices that her husband often goes out in the evening only to return at dawn, she will call the neurotuner. And this specialist (aided by the individual optical formula for his eyes noted in the marriage contract) will tune the nerves of her straying husband, who will again look at his wife as he did on their wedding day: the emotion that had begun to play off key will be returned to harmony, while the tuner, having collected his five francs, will pack up his instruments and ring the bell next door."

Katafalaki wanted to say something, but it was hard to speak with his mouth agape.

"What's more," his garrulous guest went on, "my optico-acoustical key can both tighten the pegs and loosen them. Imagine you have fallen in love with an unworthy woman who has bewitched you with her beauty. She flirts with every man she meets. To her, you are a number; to you, she is all. You have squandered half a fortune on her. Her beauty has entrapped you, as in a cage. Your nerves are stretched to breaking point. You are close to suicide. You try to drown your shameful passion in drink. But even in your drunken haze, and in your dreams—there she is. Your friends plead with you to renounce her image. All in vain. Then in walks a modest man with a metal travelling case. He takes out his instruments, seats you in a chair, like so—and fifteen minutes later you may go calmly off to meet your temptress: you will see an indescribable fright from whom you cannot get away fast enough. The optico-acoustical key has done its work. Your fortune is safe—your life too. And all for a few francs, silly even to mention it."

"But I find that hard to believe," mumbled Katafalaki, trying to be as tactful as possible, lest he offend his guest. "I cannot imagine the person or thing that would make me—after meeting a girl who seemed, or no, who *was* exquisite—shy away from her the next day in horror. That is inconceivable."

"And yet it is so. And if you have the time . . ."

"Certainly, but at seven o'clock I have a rendezvous with a lady."

"All the better. My key will make you stay a good twenty paces away from her."

"But that's . . ."

"Don't worry: a reverse turn of the key—and the fright will again be a beauty. Oh, my apparatus can douse and kindle beauty at the flick of a switch."

"Extraordinary!"

Half an hour later Katafalaki was sitting in the experimenter's chair. His eyes were covered with a black kerchief ("the tuning rays are too powerful," he was told, "they must be filtered"), while in his ears—plugged with something strange—he heard a scraping and ringing. "Voilà!" The kerchief was pulled off, and Katafalaki saw on the wall clock: half past six. Without listening to any explanations, he raced out the door. Together with the earplugs and kerchief, he banished the very thought of all those mysterious manipulations to which he had agreed to subject himself purely out of a desire to shorten the interminable wait. Now the joy of a rendezvous was near, and Katafalaki could think of nothing else.

On entering the Parc Monceau, he scurried past Chopin musing over his marble keyboard and turned toward a bust that showed white against the willows wafting over a pool: Maupassant. Two minutes to seven. On the far bench sat *she*: Gorgis recognized her dress from the day before, and her parasol, whose open silk hid her face and shoulders. He was within twenty paces when, skipping ahead with his voice, he softly called out. The parasol slid down, and at once Katafalaki, as if he had knocked into an invisible wall, took a step, then another and a third back. That optico-acoustical key—damn it!—was in perfect working order: there on the bench, smiling with thick lips and buck teeth the color of straw overhung by a long sweaty nose, sat, flirtatiously crumpling a cambric handkerchief in red webbed fingers, a monster. As Katafalaki seemed not to recognize it, the monster first nodded the stringy hemp that stuck out from behind its jug ears, then got up and, on horrible heavy-boned ankles, started toward him.

"I've come to give you my consent."

In the woman's voice there was something of yesterday's timber (any family resemblance between the two sisters ended there). Katafalaki began to regain his composure: he recalled the hero of Gozzi's *Serpent Woman*,[13] and Tagore's *Chitra*,[14] and decided to be strong. Above all, his bride mustn't know there was something wrong with his eyes. One reverse turn of the optical key and . . . He mustn't forfeit a lifetime of happiness because of a moment's tribulation. That is why, forcing a broad smile, he said:

"You look especially lovely today."

Red stubby fingers shook his hand in gratitude. Katafalaki seized this chance to say good-bye, and hustled out of the park.

A quarter of an hour later he was rapping on M. Louis's door. No one came. The gingerly rapping finger became a wildly banging fist. Silence. Puzzled, Katafalaki went downstairs to the concierge: M. Louis had gone away for a few days to Dijon. The tribulation was dragging on. A second act was being added to *Chitra*. Katafalaki waited, but events did not: the banns were published, a sewing machine was running up the trousseau; meanwhile the owner of the optical key had not returned. During trysts with his betrothed, Katafalaki sometimes tried to parry: he would sit down beside her and discreetly turn or look away, but the long glossy nose pursued him, as a magnetic needle does its pole. In the end, Katafalaki learned not to be afraid and to bear with resignation the tender gaze of his bride's mole eyes. In his pocket he had a telegram from M. Louis promising a prompt return and reversal; now he viewed his future wife's face the way a surgical patient does his soon-to-be-removed ulcer or tumor. A day sooner, a day later, perhaps even better later . . . Better later . . . To the breast of Katafalaki's frockcoat they pinned a *fleur d'orange*, while a finger on his right hand was slipped into a ring.

The day after the wedding saw the arrival, at long last, of M. Louis. He was still in traveling dress when Katafalaki burst into his room. The neurotuner surveyed him and shook his head:

"You hardly look like a newlywed."

"That depends entirely on you . . . Switch on your optical whatsit, or . . ."

"But I haven't unpacked my things.

"I'll help you."

Katafalaki's voice and manner betrayed extreme impatience. The sham inventor could not bear the gaze of his fiery eyes:

"I'm afraid my apparatus was somewhat damaged en route. It has lost accuracy. Should anything unforeseen occur—an aberration, wave interference, double vision on the retina—I am not responsible."

But the patient was already seated in the neurotuner's chair, eyes and ears awaiting blindfold and plugs.

When the manipulations were done and Katafalaki jumped up to go, Louis caught him by the elbow.

"My key has returned your wife's beauty. The surface. The dust on her wings. But the butterfly has flitted away to Mildiou. Mark my words."

Two minutes later Katafalaki sprang into a motorcar. In another few minutes the car had stopped by the house where Mildiou lived. Katafalaki raced up the steps and dashed open the door. It admitted him to a front hall. At first he heard nothing but his own uneven breathing. Then through the wall came a cascade of familiar oriolish laughter. Pressing a hand to his shattered heart, Katafalaki peeked into the room: swaying on Guy's knee, like a bird on a branch, happy eyes gleaming blue, sat his Chitra. She had shed her ugliness and, incidentally, her blouse. No! Better a long sweaty nose and jagged yellow teeth than perfidious beauty! "Ingrate!" Katafalaki wanted to scream, but just then she kissed the tip of Guy's curled moustache and said:

"I'm so grateful to that Katafalaki of yours for being such a fool. If not for him . . ."

The scream stuck in Gorgis's throat. Grasping at the wall with his palms, he let himself out and pulled the door gently to. What could he do? He felt he didn't have the strength to go on. The motorcar, still idling at the curb, received him on rumbling cushions and whisked him home. Deep in gloomy thought, Katafalaki clicked open the lock of his deserted abode. But how strange! From the bedroom shone a strip of light. He stopped, and listened. A familiar, oriolish voice was singing: "*Chacun avec sa chacune.*"* A mystical chill riffled the roots of Gorgis's hair. He wanted to back away, toward the door, but in the semidarkness his elbow struck a vase, shards spattered, and in the illuminated square appeared, her long phosphorescent— so it seemed to him—nose glistening, his wife's double.

An explanation followed. Badly frightened by her husband's distraught and contorted face, the double, tears dripping off the end of her nose, confessed everything and promised—in exchange for absolution—undying love. So Katafalaki forgave her: "chacun avec sa chacune." But the merry carousel of Paris boulevards, the whirl of bright ties and veiled carmine smiles, had begun to nettle him. From under every round boater, laughter rounded. Poor Katafalaki suddenly longed for a city of less mirthful denizens, where smiles were caulked with cigars, where houses and people were cowled in fog, while gesticulation drowsed in the depths of sixteen million pockets. Moreover, the ring on his finger reminded him of the need to work. The modest sum recovered from the sale of the late Vitsling's weather-predicting equipment was nearly gone. Gorgis did not want to touch his wife's dowry. One morning, while rummaging in a wardrobe, he dragged out his dusty case of dentistry tools. The long pliers, bent like a parrot's beak, were already covered with rust. Katafalaki dipped a chamois cloth in emery and set about scrubbing them. As he knelt over the clanking case, he imagined the strolls his needles, pliers, pincers, and tweezers would take along the firm semicircles

---

* (French) To each his own.

of British jaws; with a musing squint, he pictured a plethora of gums blooming—under the damp of fog and rain—with gumboils, caries, fistulas, and peonies of inflamed tissue.

A week later Gorgis Katafalaki, with his wife and dental instruments, crossed La Manche.

9

Since the day of Katafalaki's transformation into a London resident, four months had passed. And although thirty-two multiplied by eight million afforded a novice dentist two hundred and fifty-six million opportunities, the leather chair awaiting calls and patients on the ninth floor of a building on Commercial Road collected only dust. The police found this thinly documented doctor from abroad suspect; as for the patients, after his first failed attempt to manage the canine tusk of a strapping lad driven by pain up to the ninth floor, the dentist found himself minus several of his own front teeth. The fee, as resistant as the canine, never visited Gorgis's empty pockets. Soon his case of instruments, sold off at half price, was empty as well. The hooks on his coatrack stuck out like the branches on a leafless tree. His wife's dowry was melting away. The day the last teaspoons, tinkling pitiful good-byes, were taken to the pawnshop, his wife confessed that she was with child. The poor man clutched at his head. Life, with the art of an experienced dentist, was extracting the last pennies from his yawning pockets.

He had to think of a solution. Katafalaki spent whole days wandering amid the sparkling shop windows, the wail of newsboys, and the rubber whoosh of wheels. Eleven thousand London streets played hide-and-seek with his discombobulated steps. On steamship-agency posters, the blue-painted smoke offered the choice of any meridian. Looming through the fog, the letters on signboards promised coffee from India, fabrics from Persia, frozen meat from China, movies from Russia, fruit from Argentina, philosophy from Germany, perfume from France, jazz bands from Africa. It seemed that the air of the whole world, sucked into this gigantic humming fan, wanted to churn through it. Stock-exchange slates featured columns of numbers, while over the asphalt, as if in pursuit of a one, zerolike wheels whirled. It all resembled a rich banquet table round which delicacies were being handed with such speed you never managed to take anything. The trick was to hold out your plate in time. Katafalaki tried.

A lucky idea popped into his head just as he threw it back to survey the dusky building of the Bank of England then barring his way. The businessmen who spent their days in the City's narrow lanes had long ago dubbed that stern stone pile the Old Lady of Threadneedle Street. Today, as every day for centuries past, that stingy old lady—windowless, every fitted stone fastened—was arching her flat disgruntled brows. Dingy with soot and firmly entrenched, she seemed loath to part with even ten pence of the billions hidden under her granite hem for a pass to the baths.

But Katafalaki had already turned his back on her: his sudden idea had set his feet in motion and, steering them this way then that, practically thrust him through a narrow doorway on Fleet Street. A clerk, drowsing under the sign SUBSCRIPTIONS, looked up: "At your service." The idea, clinging to the edges of words, began slowly but stubbornly to clamber out of Katafalaki's head.

10

Mr. Keipsmyle had come out to walk his Doberman. Chiswick Park, whose treetops showed green a hundred paces from his house on King Street, was the perfect place for such a stroll. Neat sandy paths, skirting the lawns, ran down to the foggy Thames, then circled back toward the bronze gates on King Street. The air was clear and mild, and Mr. Keipsmyle, hands clasped behind his back, was whistling. His whistling, directed at the dog chasing after sparrows, kept reverting to the realm of pure music in an attempt to render something like "A Fine Old English Gentleman, One of the Olden Time": Keipsmyle was in a good mood. A newsboy darted across the path calling out the headlines, and the gentleman's fingers had reached into a vest pocket when suddenly, from around a distant bend, there appeared a figure who took the entire attention of both dog and master. The dog, sparrows forgotten, cocked its ears and began to bark at the man's big stick; his master left off whistling and peered intently. The wayfarer's staff stumped slowly over the sand, trailing two feet shod in heavy walking boots; on one knee, numbers jolting, a pedometer flashed; from his belt swung a hipflask; slung over one shoulder was a mass of sturdy footgear; only his down-tilted face was invisible under the wide brim of his faded hat. Mr. Keipsmyle beckoned to the figure—the down-tilted brim did not look up. Mr. Keipsmyle called out: "Hey, boots!" The boots turned a dozen double soles on him and disappeared down a side path. Intrigued by this strange vendor, Mr. Keipsmyle went after him, quickening his pace and raising his voice. The wayfarer stopped his staff.

"Now, listen," said Keipsmyle, breathing hard, "if that's how you treat customers, you'll have to wear out all those boots on your back yourself."

"I intend to," came the reply.

Keipsmyle glanced at the stranger's worn clothes and wearily bent shoulders, then shifted his gaze to the pedometer.

"Oho! Perhaps a shoe company has hired you to test the strength of their new soles?"

The wayfarer said nothing. He wiped the sweat from his haggard face and stumped off, but Mr. Keipsmyle, who had a kind heart, caught the poor man by his sleeve:

"Hmm, a hard occupation. But what can you do: the fish offered a worm must learn to digest hooks, or else . . ."

Whistling to his dog, he added:

"We could stop by a pub. Just near here. I'd like to offer you a bite to eat and a glass of whisky. In your place I shouldn't refuse."

The wayfarer nodded gratefully and asked:

"Is the pub on King Street?"

"Yes, on King Street."

"On the right side of the street?"

"No, on the left."

"Then forgive me, I can't join you."

"But why. It's no distance at all."

The wayfarer, smiling sheepishly, hitched up a shoulder and extracted from an inside pocket a tattered map of London dotted with notes and numbers:

"For you, perhaps. But I would have to go the long way round—11,326 miles. I'm choosing the shortest route. Therefore, Sir, much as I don't wish to offend you, I must still . . ."

Turning seven pairs of soles on his interlocutor, the mysterious stranger continued on his way. Keipsmyle, who had forgotten to close his mouth, kept a keen eye on the receding figure: first he made straight for the exit and then, ten paces shy of the gates, turned down a right-hand path; having circled a side lawn clockwise, the figure made a zigzag, came out onto the sandy main walk, and strode quickly along its right side to the end, only to double back along its left; from there he retraced the zigzag, and was lost to sight among the green splotches of trees. Keipsmyle lingered a minute more and was about to be off when suddenly he again saw the wide-stepping staff and the mass of boots on the bent back; they proceeded around the same side lawn, but counterclockwise, then cut across the main walk right in front of the fuddled gentleman and began describing arcs and zigzags along the paths crisscrossing the left-hand part of Chiswick Park.

Mr. Keipsmyle exchanged glances with his Doberman. The dog's cocked ears seemed to express a similar bewilderment.

"Every man has a fool in his sleeve."

The dog wagged its tail: hmm.

With that, they quickly left the park.

11

A thought, of course, can easily become muddled in the convolutions of a brain . . .

But if Keipsmyle had managed to peruse the morning papers before he met the wayfarer, he would not have had to experience that feeling most aptly called the fury of incomprehension.

In fact, the zigzags of the mysterious wayfarer, in whom the reader will have recognized Gorgis Katafalaki, were in fulfillment of an agreement signed on Fleet Street by the seller of an idea—Katafalaki—and its buyer—a skimpy newssheet looking for ways to increase subscriptions. Katafalaki's proposal, in essence, was this: London's eleven thousand streets, if laid end to end (in the sort of mental exercise guidebooks recommend), would encircle half the globe; "thus, if one were to walk down every street in the English capital on the right side and up every street on the left, one could go around the world without leaving the city limits." The author of this simple calculation was offering his soles to make a round-the-world journey via London.

The editorial board conferred and concurred that this project was not without merit. It would innervate the patriotic reflex, it would project Great London as the Greatest, and Londonize the world. At the same time, it would lend a coziness to the concept of "the world," bringing it right up to the city's stone walls; the equator wound round London like a wire round a spool, that's comfy, and that, by golly, should appeal to the suburbs and boost circulation. The editor spent the evening inventing a headline, and come morning Katafalaki's idea coupled with his gray-and-white portrait had been distributed to all street corners. The idea was snapped up, and in the interval between morning and evening editions, Gorgis was the most popular man in London. The newssheet launched a subscription drive meant to reward this brave experiment with a round sum. London old-timers, homebodies, and patriots reacted with enthusiasm to the call. The prize money would await Katafalaki at journey's end; meanwhile, the modest advance was just enough to provide for his wife and to buy the boots indispensable to his battle with space.

One summer morning (this event may be found in English newspapers from 1914), Gorgis Katafalaki made his start. Sporting officials, a military band, and a crowd of curiosity seekers had gathered by the main pavilion of the Royal Observatory. Katafalaki, all kitted up, stood by, treading the Earth's prime meridian with his first pair of boots. The starter raised his flag. Silence fell. The flag flicked the air—and Katafalaki took his first step. The band struck up the national anthem, and a hundred hats turned somersaults in the air. A minute later the wayfarer's back disappeared into the streets of Deptford, and the crowd began to disperse. During the first few days, the editors kept sportsmen and patriots informed of the whereabouts and momentum of the man walking from London to London via London. Katafalaki, who read the papers en route, could learn that yesterday evening he had crossed La Manche by way of Waterloo Bridge and the Victoria Embankment, while now he was traversing the fields of France, hugging the right side of Fellows Road. These notices quickened Katafalaki's steps and imagination: a few weeks later, as he was nearing the spurs of the Alps striated by the defiles between the City's stone cliffs, he asked a cobbler to stud a pair of his boots with hobnails, the better to make the ascent. Two weeks after that, when he came out onto the deserted Hungarian steppe extending down the right side of Piccadilly, he kept raising a palm to his brow as he peered through the crowds, scanning the horizon for a single soul. The London fogs, in depriving things of their clear outlines, proved marvelous helpers in this matter. Not so the people. The friendly newssheet, which at first had mentioned the wanderer, soon moved on to other, newer sensations. Like its readers, it now had no time for Katafalaki and his itinerary. The Sarajevo gunshot,[15] multiplying with the speed of proliferating infusorians, soon produced a generation of millions of gunshots known as the war. The anthem that had so recently sent Katafalaki on his way now rang out at every crossroad, vying with the clatter of wheels trundling weapons and ammunition. But whenever they met, the anthem seemed not to recognize Katafalaki and turned its brass trumpets away from his reminiscent smile. People who bumped into the wanderer and his stick mumbled their excuses and rushed on. But Katafalaki, striding via London out of London, had gone too far from the British capital to care about it: he had already crossed the Thames two hundred times by way of its nineteen bridges—it had been now the Loire, now the Seine, the Rhine, the Vistula, the Pripyat, the Dnieper, the Don, the Volga.

Ten months into his journey, the marks on his map led him down Nelson Street, a stone's throw from Commercial Road. Turning his head to the left, Katafalaki could see a familiar window on the ninth floor of a familiar building, high above the roofs of the neighboring houses. The glass suddenly glittered, the balcony door opened: by the railing, rocking a white blotch, was a hazy female figure. Katafalaki's heart beat faster: would that he could go round the corner, run up the stairs, and kiss the eyes and brow of his firstborn. Aching with the joy of fatherhood, he smiled beatifically, closed his eyes, and slumped against a wall. Something thumped right by his feet. He opened his eyes: a spare pair of boots had broken loose and leapt down onto the pavement—seemingly ready, ahead of their owner, to race as fast as their soles would carry them up to his wife and child. This coincidence sobered the wayfarer: he retethered the refractory boots, slung them over his shoulder, and again his staff stumped off along the predetermined zigzag. Katafalaki was not one to go astray: the line plotted on his city-world map was to him like the tightrope stretched over an abyss: one false step would cross everything out.

This happened on the High Street where it cuts through the Borough, not far from the old belfry of St. George's. A baker's boy, balancing two round cartons of raisin cakes on his head, reread the customers' addresses and made for London Bridge. He had barely left St. George's behind on his right when it began to rain: first a few inquisitive drops rapped on the cartons, as if to ask what was inside. The boy picked up his pace—the rain began to drum on the cardboard lids with a thousand fingers, attempting to get at the raisins by force. Raisins and boy ducked under an entrance awning. At that, the furious rain crashed down onto the asphalt and, helped by the wind, tried with its wet tongue to reach the elusive treats. But the boy had dashed inside and was making funny faces at the rain while surveying the deserted street: as far as he could see, it was completely empty, save for the spur stones and a dustman's cart abandoned in the middle of the pavement, and he was beginning to feel bored when suddenly there appeared, off to the left, through the verticals of rain, a moving shape. Blurry at first through the streaming window, the shape, forcing its way through the rain-lashed air with a long stick, trudged stubbornly into view. Now one could say with near certainty that it was a man and that he had a hump on his back; another fifteen seconds, and the baker's boy let out a whoop: "Not a hump, boots!"—and when the figure came closer still, he counted: four pairs. In five or six more seconds, he could try to shout over the rain; he threw open the entrance door and waved:

"Sir! If it's a shower you want, where's your washcloth and soap?"

Without even a glance in the direction of the shout, the figure went on severing the watery threads with his staff. Then the boy, sticking his cropped head out from under the awning, took his highest treble note:

"Hey, listen, you, whatever your name is! Don't you know Mr. Cloudburst likes to go about alone? He doesn't need escorts."

The figure shambled past him, and the annoyed boy could see only eight receding funnels fastened to his back and sloshing water. The boy made one last effort, yelling till he was hoarse:

"The devil take you! If you're selling water in leather bottles, then why aren't they corked?!"

But the wanderer had been curtained by the rain, and the boy, admitting defeat, went back inside, wiping drops of water and sweat from his face.

■ □ ■

One day in the autumn of 1915, when the main imports were corpses from Ypres, and crosses in London graveyards had to squeeze together, Mr. Broomes and his ten-year-old granddaughter stood by a path in Ilford Cemetery watching the work of four shovels over seven feet of earth. The seven feet obtruded their fat, clayey belly higher and higher; once more the shovels, metal palms gently ringing, smoothed over the grave's narrow groin; the back of one palm patted down a damp round roll. Mr. Broomes paid up, put on his hat, and took Maddy by the hand:

"Come on."

"Grandfather."

"What, Maddy?"

"Daddy's gone to heaven, right?"

"Yes."

"Is it far?"

"Very."

"Farther than Tower Street?"

"Farther."

"Farther than Edgeware Road?"

"Much farther."

"Grandfather, where's that man going?"

"What man? Watch your feet, it's muddy—you could slip."

"Why does he have so many boots on his back?"

"I don't know. I suppose he has a long way to go. Do watch out— there's a puddle."

Crosses upon crosses. They were almost at the archway gates.

"Grandfather."

"Now what is it?"

"Maybe he's going to heaven too. Would three pairs of boots be enough?"

"Hmm."

"Grandfather, I'll run and ask him to tell Daddy that you and I . . ."

"Don't be silly."

"But you said . . ."

"Mind the step. Hello, John. City Road. Maddy, cover your mouth with your scarf—against the wind. There."

The motorcar swung round the entrance circle and proceeded down the long thoroughfare that is Romford Road. Within a few minutes John had turned on the headlamps: it was growing dark. The car was already winding through the streets of Finsbury when from under the scarf a pair of small, sad lips peeked out:

"But why did he walk in such a strange way: forward, then back, then forward, and back again, and . . .?"

"Who? Ah, that man. I don't know."

"Grandfather, maybe he was lost."

"I told you—keep your mouth covered: it's windy."

The motorcar rolled out onto a City Road resplendent with lights.

■ □ ■

It so happened that on Twelfth Night of 1916 the line of Katafalaki's route lay along Fleet Street. It was the hour when offices finished work and clerks locked away their ledgers. Katafalaki plodded down the street of newspapers, peering in the windows. Now here was that door behind which they had traded him his idea for a hard and long journey . . . The wayfarer's cheeks were sunken, his pockets empty; in his straggly beard, icicles glittered. Through the glass door, he could see moving figures. Katafalaki stood for a minute, wavering: he didn't want to ask for mercy or even help, but all his joints ached, while hunger gnawed at his gut. Yes, he had no choice, he must ask for some small sum against his eventual prize. They must understand. He was about to open the door when he noticed that between him and it lay the street: the office was on the other side. He was twenty steps from money, but those steps would lead him astray; his route ran along the left side—the money was luring him to the right. No, better not to arrive than to cross over. Katafalaki faced round and continued on his way. The pedometer accreted to his leg had amassed such a load of numbers and miles that every bend of his knees cost him the utmost effort.

■ □ ■

The autumn of 1916 brought London a great many trials. German submarines were breaking through the minefields and nosing up the Thames. From above, airships threatened. At night London doused its lights, and the streets were as dark and peopleless as in the days of Mr. Pickwick. About eleven o'clock one evening, a policeman stood on a corner of the long street that frames the parallelogram of the West India Docks. It was so quiet that he could hear the ticking of his watch under the fourth button of his uniform. No wonder the sudden sound of footsteps a hundred yards off put him on his guard: a thief or a drunk? For a drunk the sound was too steady and at the same time soft: therefore . . . The policeman let the footsteps come ten steps closer then pressed the knob on his electric torch. The man, stopped by the bolt of light, stood with both hands resting on a staff; slung over his shoulder, heavy duckbilled toes down, were two pairs of boots. Well yes, of course. The policeman, barring the way with his truncheon, brought his torch closer still to the tramp's face. Their eyes met. The expression that flickered from brow to chin of the policeman was of a kind rarely seen under a helmet. The truncheon sank down, the torch retrieved its beam, and Gorgis Katafalaki heard: "Be on your way."

A pair of soles and a stick stumped off in the direction of the embankment by All Saints Poplar.

■ □ ■

One night in the autumn of 1917, an apprentice at the Royal Observatory was working under the dome—wide to the stars—of the main pavilion. At the first glimmers of dawn, he finished his observations and notes, stopped the clock drive on the telescope, and made his way to the exit. Even before opening the door, he heard two voices arguing loudly and in not at all astronomical terms. One voice he recognized—it belonged to the night watchman; the other—hoarse and strained, but stubborn as a woodpecker's beak on bark—was . . . The astronomer pushed open the door to find a poor wretch slumped on the observatory steps, soles planted on the Earth's prime meridian; despite the watchman's jabs and urgings, he would not budge. Meanwhile the astronomer, having thought better of the word "soles," promptly amended it. The man seated athwart the meridian (although, again, meridians have no athwarts) was barefoot; his head, under a mat of dirty dark hair, kept nodding over his knees, on one of which, atop a torn trouser leg, glinted the number-laden disk of a pedometer. Not counting those numbers and a stick, sprawled on the stone steps with a look of extreme exhaustion, the tramp appeared to have no other baggage.

The watchman turned to the astronomer for support:

"Looks to me, sir, like a deserter from the front. Hey, Tommy," he shook the drowsing tramp by the shoulder, "if you take telescopes for guns, you're either shell-shocked, or . . . Let's see your papers."

The tramp, without opening his eyes, reached inside his rags and drew out a crumpled packet of newssheets: on one of them, circled in red pencil, the printer's ink showed a face that could have passed for that of his younger brother. Thus Katafalaki completed his round-the-world journey, never having set foot outside the British capital.

That same day he embraced his wife and, beaming with proud expectation, asked:

"And where is our firstborn?"

There were two firstborns. In his joy, the world-weary wanderer gave this no importance. But the next day he couldn't help noticing that the twins were of different ages and in most ways unalike. A furrow of suspicion inserted itself between Gorgis's arched brows. Once again tears trickled down his wife's long glossy nose; once again she confessed her deceit. Katafalaki was indignant:

"Ere those shoes were old . . ."[16] He began with that bitter quote only to remember that seven pairs of double soles had been completely worn out. But another circumstance, too, prevented him from finishing his tirade: round the door now poked a head wearing a trim ginger moustache. The head made to turn back, but Katafalaki already had it by the necktie:

"Listen here, on what grounds . . ."

"Well, you see, I'm an active member of the Philanthropic Society for the Care of Hideous Women, and since your wife . . ."

Katafalaki yanked on the necktie as if it were the bellpull for a divorce lawyer.

"You're lying," he cried, causing the lips to turn paler than the moustache. "I've walked up and down every street in London, I've seen every signboard for every association, every society, every firm, and not one of them was for a . . . How dare you!"

By now the philanthropist's necktie sooner recalled the twine that fishermen thread through the flapping gills of a caught fish. Yet there was something that distinguished this victim of an enraged husband from a fish: the victim refused to be silent—and through his necktie noose he squeezed out these words:

"I'm an Obr."

"A what?!" said Gorgis, his curiosity piqued even in that moment.

"Obr. Brr . . . Another inch and my tongue would have been hanging out: *Pogibosha aki obry.** What sort of a Russian are you if you don't know that ancient Russian saying?! Actually," the necktie had slipped from Katafalaki's limp fingers, "that saying is not entirely correct—not *all* the Obrs[17] perished. Indeed *I* am the last Obr. My death would mean the death of an entire people. Which is why I must be fruitful and multiply: so that the ancient Obr tribe does not die out and the legend does not become a reality."

Katafalaki felt extremely disconcerted. How could he, an inveterate supporter of national minorities, raise a hand against the last Obr? He offered the Obr people, so nearly decimated a second time, a hospitable armchair, and they both, host and guest, began to discuss how to refute that lamentable saying. The first thing to do was to increase the number of little Obrs; the little Obrs would grow into big Obrs, and then . . . But for the little Obrs to grow, they must be fed. Katafalaki would feed them. Yes, but to feed them, he must have money. Katafalaki leapt up and dashed off to the offices of the newssheet holding his prize. The familiar door on Fleet Street admitted a man with a delightedly excited face; an hour later it closed on a man with a face ruefully long: the promised sum had been embezzled a year ago by the newssheet's paymaster. The one consolation to the man who had walked all that way was that his swindler now sat in prison.

But Katafalaki would have been a bad Obrphile if he had immediately abandoned his plan. The London papers were devoting copious ink to the Russian Revolution then threatening to overflow the dykes of its borders. Katafalaki began to follow events. It became

---

* (Old Church Slavonic) They perished like the Obrs—i.e., to the last man.

clear that the list of republics and autonomous regions incorporated into Soviet Russia was only getting longer and more complex. One day, while poring over a newspaper on a bench in Trafalgar Square, Katafalaki slapped his forehead with such force that a passing vendor of copperware looked back to see if he hadn't dropped a pot: "Damn it! Why shouldn't the Obrs have one too?"

Within a few days, a blueprint for the creation of an Autonomous Republic of Obrs had been tucked inside a briefcase and under one elbow by Katafalaki, now en route from London to Moscow.

12

The first days after his arrival in Moscow were busy and brisk. Though his route, obstructed by some dozen visas, had been hard and long, now that Katafalaki and his blueprint were in that cauldron of simmering republics and autonomous regions, he had only to click open his briefcase—and the Obrrepublic would spring out onto the designated territory.

Above the Moscow snowdrifts, red one-petaled flags bloomed. The pincushion cheeks of passersby, pricked by the frost, glowed like rosy plush. Sled runners rasped over the glistening snow, like violinists' bows over rosined strings, scraping along at the pitch of C-sharp.

Katafalaki, too, scraped briskly along from door to door, "forwarding" copies of his blueprint from office to office. Alas, in the scrape of commissars' pens, scrawling a terse "reject," there was nothing bracing, while the frosty smiles of their secretaries, past whom the petitioner was never allowed, exuded a chill of hopelessness.

But Katafalaki did not give up. His Obr idea must be carried out—if not from above, then from the side. He decided to appeal to the public. The colorful posters inviting people to the Polytechnical Museum[18] made him see just what to do next: he would give a lecture—no, lectures, a series of well-publicized readings—then the higher-ups would have to reject their "reject." An hour later Katafalaki was conferring with citizen Golidze, a specialist in the organization of such gatherings. Things were looking up. Then suddenly, in a morning newspaper, Katafalaki chanced across this item: "The lecturer, Comrade Lunacharsky,[19] was met with an explosion of appl . . ." Turbid spots swam before Katafalaki's eyes. He crumpled up the icy sheet without even reading the name of that infernal substance—"applolite" or . . . What did it matter? True, the red flags that day did not have black borders. Even so Katafalaki, hardly a coward, felt he had no right to risk his idea, and his lectures never took place.

He must find another way. His habit of going for strolls, ingrained in his nerves by his London walkabout, made him poke into every Moscow cul-de-sac. To right and left stretched shop windows. A rapidly emptying purse prevented Gorgis looking inside, but from the outside those flat glass gardens bloomed with such fantastical snowy roses thick with icy thorns that the imaginations of passersby had to race to catch up. In the end, one passerby (Katafalaki, of course) managed not only to catch up, but even to outrun . . . Here is what he came up with.

Katafalaki decided to declare himself a state. After all, the great often begins from something quite small. Next morning, sticking out of a letterbox slot on a Moscow backstairs (to greet the scurrying slop buckets), was the flag of the Obrrepublic. Katafalaki well understood the duties imposed on him by his new political position. He would have to be commissar of all his commissariats and his own subject. Raising first his right hand, then his left, he elected himself to all the top posts in Obrland, whose borders extended from the entrance door to the walls of his room, hung with decrees and directives regulating the life of its inhabitant. As subject, Katafalaki paid himself (as ruler) taxes, transferring his last kopecks from one pocket to the other. Wishing to be as good as any other state, he immersed himself in a course of specialized literature: it turned out that a state builds its economic policy on external or internal debt, cancels that debt, and concludes secret treaties. Gorgis's truthful and open nature recoiled at such behavior—as subject he even tried to complain, but as ruler he put himself in prison, shutting himself up in his room under lock and key. The life of this man-state was daily becoming more and more unbearable. Katafalaki supposed that a state on the verge of collapse usually attempted to save the situation by declaring war on someone: he might have resorted to this extreme measure but, alas, in his pocket he hadn't money enough even for a postage stamp—to send a declaration of war without a stamp struck Katafalaki as discourteous and not in accord with the laws of European diplomacy. So began and ended the world's most peculiar state, the Oberrepublic, which, perhaps, will someday find its historian.

Katafalaki rose up against himself, stripped himself of all his posts, and began to search for other ways of manifesting and making sense of his existence.

■ □ ■

Before long—in a Moscow bystreet under four screws—there appeared this nameplate:

Dentist
KATAFALAKI
Entrance round the back
Discount for union members

People who had gone through the Civil War, who had learned to rap out a hungry tap dance with their chattering teeth, could not be scared off by Katafalaki's pliers. Meekly waiting their turn, they offered up their gums to the hooks and drills in his tooth-torturing office. The citizen who had just wrested himself from the pliers was promptly replaced by the next in line, while the stipple of bloody spittle that began on the top step of the backstairs trailed off around the corner on Tverskaya Street, two doors down from the Moscow City Soviet.

Everything went smoothly until the appearance of a certain strange patient. This patient turned up in the waiting room on the heels of dusk, whose gray back made it hard to discern him. Then again, the other patients—buried in their pain, cocooned in bandages, kerchiefs, and cotton wool—expressed not the least curiosity. But the wall clock, so it seemed to one patient rocking in his seat like a pendulum, began to tick and tock strangely distinctly and diligently, shooting sound and pain from tooth to brain. The chairs were emptying one by one. It was almost completely dark when, in the doorway between office and waiting room, Katafalaki himself appeared. Carrying a small case of instruments, he passed quickly down the row of empty chairs, stopping only at the last:

"Please excuse me. Urgent call. I don't have time."

"Yet I maintain," the patient barred his way, "that Time is exactly what you do possess."

Since this phrase was uttered in a patently foreign accent, Katafalaki was unsurprised by the strangeness of its construction.

"I know better," he muttered, making for the door.

"I doubt that."

"But why?"

"Because I . . . This may strike you as strange . . . I myself am, only please don't be afraid, Time."

Katafalaki took a step back.

"Forgive me, you want the nerve specialist, I am a dentist. You mistook the door."

"Not at all. You have extracted wisdom teeth?"

"Yes."

"Well then, mightn't you try to extract the very wisdom? That is, of course, more complicated. But, you see, I absolutely must have my wisdom out."

Even sober-minded Polonius after his aside, "Though this be madness,[20] yet there is method in't," is drawn willy-nilly into a series of questions. What could one expect of Katafalaki? Within a minute doctor and patient sat side by side, deep in animated conversation. The patient gave this account of himself:

"You see, the rumors about a country meddling in my affairs[21] couldn't but catch my attention. First we set the clocks ahead one hour, then two, then three, finally we began shifting centuries from one place to another: the twentieth to the twenty-fifth, and so on. I don't like it when someone mixes up my seconds, much less my epochs. To ignore this, to plead a lack of time, was for me, Time himself, alas, impossible. (In this sense I envy you, Katicktockaf-alaki.) I sprang down from my dial onto the rails and away to Moscow. On finding myself in this strange city, I naturally observed the strictest incognito. Some things at first even pleased and intrigued me—for instance, your ring roads A and B. I remember my first day, striding along those circling boulevards: I simply could not stop my soles from rapping out the seconds. That's habit for you! Yet a clock-face disk fourteen miles round did, I confess, somewhat tire me. I sat down on a boulevard bench—and that's when it all began. Next to me, legs outstretched, were two men. One yawned, while the other said: "I honestly don't know how to kill Time." I shuddered and edged away. Mustn't let on. In my head, though, the wheels were turning: it's good that simpleton doesn't know how, but what if he finds out? Half an hour had not gone by when I happened on another leisurely pair discussing how to kill me. Wherever I went, I found people plotting against my life. Where could I hide? I decided to hole up in a hotel, but on approaching the illuminated entrance I saw two men standing outside, evidently waiting for someone. Before I had stepped into the strip of light, one of them said: "Here they do nothing but waste Time." I could only retire—into the darkness of a bystreet. A hotel was not the safe place I had imagined; worse still, people had begun to recognize me. With that gloomy thought, I extended my nighttime stroll along the gradually emptying streets of your capital. Exhaustion forced me now and again to lean against a wall and then I saw above me the silent cutouts of belfries with mutely drooping bells. What I ended by thinking was this: the mechanisms that chime faith have broken and stopped; soon the mechanisms of time, too, will strike their last and stop their pendulums the world over; then they'll put me up against a wall (like so) and . . . I can't go on like this. My patience has come unwound. I want neither this nor that. Let the world not be, so long as I can beat: from all the clockfaces and watch dials. Take your pliers—and to hell with my wisdom, root and all!"

Katafalaki was shocked. Well yes, yes, of course, he must help. Since Time had fallen on such hard times . . . Words failed Katafalaki, but not actions—with him that never happened.

That night Time, traveling third class, accompanied by his protector—having swapped the whirl of clockwork wheels for the whirl of train wheels—fled to a remote halt on the Russian plain where here and there village roofs poked up like gray molehills.

The village where Katafalaki and Time sought refuge differed from most others outside Moscow: attached to every log hut was a lean-to with a fifth window, and by every fifth window sat a tockiter. These artisans, whose craft had come down through generations, were accustomed to cobbling together—from weights, patterned hands, and serrated tin—crude pendulum clocks that hobbled pell-mell after time. Working in the country hush, amid the staid ticking of their wares on the walls, lovingly decorating the clocks' white faces with garlands of violet- and pink-painted blossoms, these craftsmen knew the seconds by touch and revered their benefactor—time. It was of five such windows that Katafalaki and his mysterious companion asked for asylum. Soon the two were seated among the beards and eyes that had taken them into their close circle. Katafalaki told them in plain words what was what: the Moscow you-know-who's want to do away with time; but if there's no time, then who'll buy your clocks? If you want to hang onto your earnings, you must hide Time so that not a single eye . . .

The beards nodded: um-hmm, only where is he, Time, the good man.

"What do you mean where? He's right here in front of you."

Katafalaki's companion, smiling politely, half-rose and bowed. The peasants scratched their beards: passing strange, never seen such a thing . . . But Katafalaki, who had foreseen their hesitation, had his proof at the ready. He drew back the flap of his companion's coat: Time's entire body was hung with driving weights descending on tangled clockwork chains from shoulders to hips. The fetters of this persecuted martyr, briefly displayed to the circle of eyes, jingled for just a moment, then disappeared behind flap and buttons.

Silence reigned. Only the weight-driven clocks on the walls went on wonderingly: can't-be-can-it—can't-be—can-it. The village elder, wiping sweat from his brow, repeated after them: can be.

So Time came to live in the village, daily becoming an object of surprise to an ever-widening circle of people: he drank milk in the morning, spoke with a distinctly foreign accent, inquired about the mood in neighboring villages, made notes in his notebooks, and sent letters abroad. Then suddenly one day, Time found himself between two unbuckled holsters. His face, grown round from the country air and victuals, instantly fell, becoming long and gaunt. The villagers stared after the receding wheels[22] with much sighing and scratching of heads. Two days later, Gorgis was called in for questioning:

"Tell me," said a man in a field jacket, peering under the Gothic arches of Katafalaki's astonished eyebrows, "do you honestly believe that time, or causality, or, say . . . surplus value, may wear lisle socks and go to the dentist?"

Katafalaki said nothing, but his eyes answered. The mouth of the man in the field jacket twitched with the inkling of a smile:

"Very well. You may go. But remember: if nonsense comes to us and complains that she was whipped, you will answer, Citizen Katafalaki. Mark my words."

13

Nothing more is heard from Katafalaki after that. Whether it was his conversation with the smiling field jacket that acted on him like a moderator pedal on piano keys, or the reactions to that conversation among friends and compatriots, no one knows. He withdrew from the public and turned down his enthusiasm, like the wick of a smoking lamp. In a word, he stopped providing material for his Life. Why? Some say, because he wised up; others say, because he remarried—and twice married, once . . . Actually, that saying refers to something else.

Incidentally, about his second marriage. The woman who became his wife is, they say, terribly lazy. When Katafalaki was still trying to get a definite answer out of her ("I will" or "I will not"), she said *I will* only because it's one word shorter than *I will not*.

If that's the truth, then the truth is regrettable: clearly, Gorgis Katafalaki's wife will never write her memoirs, and the Life of one of our most remarkable contemporaries will remain unfinished.

1933

KRZHIZHANOVSKY'S NOTEBOOKS AND LOOSE-LEAF NOTES

Excerpts

TITLE: *THE BALD WOMEN'S CLUB*

■ □ ■

The only thing I know about Truth is that when we meet she does not bow.

■ □ ■

The archaeology of oneself.

■ □ ■

Marvelous adventures inside a manual of logic.

■ □ ■

Briefcase carriers.

■ □ ■

Story of a writer: first he reads, then he is read, and then they read over him.

■ □ ■

I would like to get out of my artistry (and my conscience), but can't find the door.

■ □ ■

Fairy Tale: He was a deeply venerated man. The street on which he lived was named after him. Out of modesty, he moved to another street. Then that street too was named after him. Soon every street in the city had the same name: people got all mixed up and cursed the venerated man.

■ □ ■

A spare pair of parents.

■ □ ■

To live is to put a spoke in the wheel of the hearse in which I am being carried.

■ □ ■

Saint Peter had lost his keys. He went in search. Meanwhile the righteous gathered by the gates. He found his keys and opened the gates: the righteous were fighting—as if in line for butter—in line for heaven.

■ □ ■

There once lived a king: his name was Lear. He had three daughters.

■ □ ■

Every man has a fool in his sleeve. If every one of us really does have a fool in their sleeve, then the distance from one's sleeve to the pen in one's hand is too short not to worry about literature.

■ □ ■

I, to be honest, am a little shy of myself.

■ □ ■

An exhausting respite.

■ □ ■

1. A syllogism composed of images.
   The middle image (M) appears in the image-conclusion.
2. Treat concepts as images, correlate them as images.
   These are the two principal devices in my literary experiments.

■ □ ■

An out-of-work echo.

■ □ ■

A portfolio without genius.
(And a genius without portfolio.)

■ □ ■

Intelligence has no practical use. It's about the faraway, knowing a foreign language without knowing how to obtain a passport.

It's unprofitable since it causes only pain; it humiliates the small with the great, shames the facts with ideas.

As a result, by means of selection the best adapted survive (the adapters die out), and intelligence becomes a vestige. Someday there will remain of it—as of the archaeopteryx—only a flat imprint on a few pages—and that's all.

Example—literature: "stupid, but talented." Soon: "talented and also stupid."

■ □ ■

Parody is the art of looking back while moving ahead.

■ □ ■

I live in such a distant future that my future seems to me past, spent, and turned to dust.

■ □ ■

A mind of average height.

■ □ ■

Someday they'll put me, like my pince-nez, in a case. Fine. I never really needed nearsightedness. Rather nearsightedness needs philosophers.

■ □ ■

Scoundrels, "bad guys," and the like always manage to succeed not only in life, but in plays, novels, etc. They always turn out better, artistically more convincing than the honest, kind, etc.

■ □ ■

In childhood we fear a dark room, in old age—death.
(V. Don't frighten me with a dark room—with death.)

■ □ ■

If God ever did exist, then people long ago drove him to suicide.

■ □ ■

I'm enough of a poet not to write verses.

■ □ ■

My artistic logic:

> All men are mortal.
> Kai is mortal.
> Therefore, Kai is, at least somewhat, a man.

■ □ ■

Stories for the crossed-out.

■ □ ■

I am a crossed-out person.

■ □ ■

Hamlet, the ultimate metaphysician, is sheer being: you cannot kill (nothingness, too, is shot through with dreams) the horror of eternity.

■ □ ■

People keep mulling Goethe's "Stop, moment,"[*] and its interpretations. But to my mind: if the clock has stopped, then it's broken. If "time has stopped," then it too . . . Your famous eternity—*nunc stans*[†]—is simply a broken, distorted concept of time. That's right, the clock must be taken to be mended.

■ □ ■

People go to work every day, not so their thoughts.

■ □ ■

My existence is a simple courtesy.

■ □ ■

In a vacuum everything falls at the same speed.

■ □ ■

A young man who dyes his hair gray.

---

[*] In *Faust* (Part One, ll. 1699*ff*): "If to the moment I should say: / Abide, you are so fair— / Put me in fetters on that day, / I *wish* to perish then, I swear. / Then let the death bell ever toll, / Your service done, you shall be free, / The clock may stop, the hand may fall, / As time comes to an end for me." *Goethe's Faust*, trans. Walter Kaufmann (New York: Anchor Books, 1963), 185.

[†] (Latin) The "now" standing still, per Thomas Aquinas in *Summa theologica*, part 1, question 10, article 2.

■ □ ■

We are polite, but only to the deceased. If you want to hear a heartfelt speech, die.

■ □ ■

Before sunset, the long shadows from things remind us that the day too was long, but like a shadow.

■ □ ■

We're like people who at night walk on the sunny side, thinking it's warmer there.

■ □ ■

The girl was very lazy.

"So? Will you or will you not?" he asked her. "I will," she said, only because it was one word shorter than "I will not." They married.

When it came time to give birth, she was too lazy to push. This dragged on until finally, at the urging of husband and doctor, she overcame her sloth. Into the world was born a full-grown man—with beard and moustache—like you.

■ □ ■

When I die, don't keep the nettles from growing up over me: let them sting too.

■ □ ■

Dream: my manuscripts being buried in a dustbin.

■ □ ■

War. Death works without a moment's respite. Death dies of exhaustion.

■ □ ■

Yes, we are the salt of the earth, but . . . loaded onto an ass.

■ □ ■

Even if thinking is determined by being, no agreements were ever signed between the two: over the head of the headless (i.e., being) thinking speaks only to truth.

■ □ ■

We all live on Unwitting Street.

■ □ ■

What men die by.

■ □ ■

My consciousness is a cart track through existence (a clearing cut in existence).

■ □ ■

My only guests: thoughts.

■ □ ■

You and I will meet in nothingness.

■ □ ■

Handmade hope.

■ □ ■

The nonsense of sense.

■ □ ■

Time, driven into a watch and put on a chain, like a dog (in a vest pocket).

■ □ ■

Taken from life at a ticket office:
"I'm first."
"No, I am!"
"Comrades, don't quarrel. Save your strength for building socialism."

■ □ ■

Case № . . . The Eviction of Conscience from Literature.

■ □ ■

Life is a silly agonizing insomnia.

■ □ ■

Fairy Tale: The devil leases the world from God. But doesn't obey God's laws.

■ □ ■

When enemy agents are circling over culture, the lights in heads must be turned out.

■ □ ■

Here the outskirts of literature ended. I went as far as possible past the line of words, walked through wastelands, falling down and picking myself up, despairing and spurred by the power of my despair. Suddenly I saw—looming up through the nothingness—the verge of a forest of mysterious and ineffable images. I looked round—and realized: I would never make it back to words.

■ □ ■

My thoughts came together in syllogisms, then fanned out into a line of conclusions and silently approached the exposition. There—beyond the barbed and barricaded dusk—lay the land of conceptions.

■ □ ■

A thinker is not someone who thinks loyally, but someone who is loyal to his thoughts.

■ □ ■

"Pack up your thoughts and be ready at a moment's notice to move into a new worldview."

■ □ ■

My life in two parts:

1) a lost chess match,
2) analysis of that loss.

■ □ ■

I'm dead. I can hear the grass growing up over me. Still, that's better than hearing the slaps in my face.

■ □ ■

Passengers on a train argue about the window ("open or closed") as if they were Slavophiles and Westernizers, and the window were the "window to Europe."

■ □ ■

The most loathsome thing in the world: the thoughts of a genius living out their days in the head of a mediocrity.

■ □ ■

Alcohol's mistress: Boredom.

■ □ ■

Wit and paradoxicalness come from a squint-eyed intellectual vision. Logic with a slight squint. Someday (under socialism) they will cure this.

■ □ ■

An Englishman, before cutting his throat with a razor, will shave with it.

■ □ ■

Duels (war): the art of killing politely.

■ □ ■

I suffer from my logicality as from a disease. Cure me of my logic!

■ □ ■

Revolution is a speeding up of facts, which outrun thought.

■ □ ■

The slowest process is the process of thinking a thought through to its muscle, of turning that thought into deed.

■ □ ■

Only exceptional people create rules.

■ □ ■

I would rather create rules than follow them.

■ □ ■

Impatience—that is my essence. Yet life demands of me the greatest patience.

■ □ ■

There is no God, yet his name is everywhere. Even in the speeches of our leaders—side by side with "you see" and "so to speak."

■ □ ■

I live on the margins of a book called *Society*.

■ □ ■

Yes, I love myself; but it seems my love is unrequited.

■ □ ■

A suicide goes to fetch death. Death in the guise of the local doctor. Death is out. The suicide waits. Falls asleep.

■ □ ■

When death is so rude as to make people wait—that is called sickness.

■ □ ■

Try to get along in the mountains and in learning without guides.

■ □ ■

I have a platform ticket to literature. I watch others seeing people off or departing. But I'm not meeting anyone or seeing anyone off. That's how it is.

■ □ ■

"What are you doing?"
"Enriching nonexistence."

■ □ ■

Death and its environs.
(Life = the environs of death.)

■ □ ■

My role as a failure in this world bores and wearies me not as an actor, but as a spectator.

■ □ ■

A clock hand that recoils from the future and moves counterclockwise (to think counterclockwise).

■ □ ■

I did not know that one could, to such a degree, not exist.

■ □ ■

Friends as a particularly dangerous variety of enemy.

■ □ ■

A person, insofar as he is a person, is always a bridge. One person is a pole across a stream; another is a rickety catwalk; yet another is a steep arc over a deep channel; and then there are the two-, three-, and five-span ornate people-bridges on concrete piers. People-bridges from today to tomorrow, people along whom the way is closed to pedestrians. People from epoch to epoch and, finally, from oneself to oneself (the greatest distance of all).

■ □ ■

Truth as the plaintiff.

■ □ ■

I'm a foreign tourist in life.
It's time I repatriated to nonexistence.

■ □ ■

We all stand a little aloof from ourselves.

■ □ ■

The art of *seeing* concepts.

■ □ ■

The writer as a variety of person.

■ □ ■

I'm not on good terms with the present day, but posterity loves me.

■ □ ■

A combination of biology and mathematics, a mixture of microorganisms and infinitesimals—that is my logical element.

■ □ ■

To the disorder of the day.

■ □ ■

Dream: my darling and I are approaching London. But the train loses its way among the switches and stops somewhere on the outskirts of the city's outskirts. We collect our things; we'll have to make our way to the city on foot. It's nearly evening. Everything looks like an etching. Yellow chains of lamps. I talk to her about the strange graphite quality. I already vaguely suspect its overly generalized nature—from my eyes, not to them—of not existing. But my darling says: "This is a London particular.* It's all right, we'll get there." With the toe of my shoe I knock (by accident) into a bush: at first it's a cloud of dust, and then it too dissolves like so many dust motes into nothingness. I feel a strange anguish: we won't get there; before we do, something will happen. I set down my suitcase and say: "I think I'm about to wake up." She says: "But what about me? If you go away to reality, what will I do?" She catches me by the hand, I see tears in her eyes, but I can't go on: I rest my head in her hands, my dream is in its death agony. I dimly see the receding image of my darling and . . . die into reality.

■ □ ■

I drink because every bout is a tiny model of life (*l'eau de vie*†): first the anticipation of "vie"—then an adolescent excitement—then a

---

* A term for the thick smog caused by soot particulates; used by Dickens in *Bleak House* and described by T. S. Eliot in "The Love Song of J. Alfred Prufrock" ("The yellow fog that rubs its back upon the window-panes, The yellow smoke that rubs its muzzle on the window-panes").

† (French) Brandy. Literally: the water of life.

youthful sober-drunk sensation, the emergence of erotic images—then a feeling of inertia, glass after glass, maturity with its speeding up of time—then lethargy, muddled thoughts, drowsiness, indifference—this is decrepitude, old age, and, finally, senility, mental decay, the unfinished glass, satiety—and, at last, a dreamless sleep, death . . . And all this in twenty minutes.

■ □ ■

The days are being driven back into the past, but they are resisting.

■ □ ■

Logic for children.

■ □ ■

The adventures of a syllogism.

■ □ ■

"A length of time": a shop that sells time—time measured off by the yard and cut to order. ("I stood in line for two hours to get a minute" and so on.)

■ □ ■

To think is to differ in opinion with oneself.

■ □ ■

Time—from time to time—sits down to rest.

■ □ ■

To object to nonexistence bearing down on me is useless. Can a footprint in the sand argue with the wind?

■ □ ■

Humor is the trait that separates people of a higher mental order from those of a lower one. All people can be divided into two halves: this side of humor and the far side. Humor is the mind's good weather. On gloomy days it's harder to work.

■ □ ■

A lively, sincere pessimism is more joyful than a forced optimism. (V. A healthy pessimism is somehow jollier than a sickly, formal optimism.)

■ □ ■

TITLE: *MR. ELLIPSIS*

■ □ ■

A pocket dictionary of Shakespeare's puns. (As an article.)

■ □ ■

When a person espies the humorous side of the process of coming to know the truth, he abandons his philosophical lookout and turns to art; he appeals all concepts in the Court of Images.

AFTERWORD

Through the Eyes of a Friend
(Material for a Life of Sigizmund Krzhizhanovsky):
Excerpts

ANNA BOVSHEK[1]

All my hard life I have been a literary nonbeing, honestly working
for being.

► Sigizmund Krzhizhanovsky

KIEV

Kiev. 1920. I'm walking down the street past a solid wall of snow and
trees white with frost. The street is nearly deserted. Now and then
one hears an alarming clatter of hooves: a lone horsemen gallops
past, or a whole detachment of riders. By the look of them—in wide
red pants, with topknots on their heads and lances tilted forward; in
shaggy black hats; or in gray greatcoats and peaked caps with a five-
pointed star—one can tell who holds power in the city: Petlyura's
forces, the Whites, or the Reds. Passing the Conservatory, I notice
nailed to the door a small printed announcement:

S. D. Krzhizhanovsky

Lectures and conversations about art

First series (6 lectures)

1.	Thursday 1 March	The culture of mystery in art
2.	Monday 5	Art and "art"
3.	Thursday 8	The created creator (J. Erigena)[2]
4.	Monday 12	Drafts. Analysis of the crossed-out
5.	Thursday 15	Poetry and chaos
6.	Monday 19	The problem of performance

The lectures will be held in the Conservatory hall at half past eight. Series subscription: 500 rubles.

I had often heard about Krzhizhanovsky, his lectures, his discussions of music. Everyone said they were interesting. Indeed, this series intrigued me. I should go and, if possible, be introduced to the lecturer; but I don't have five hundred rubles. I could stop by the Conservatory, where I'd almost certainly run into an acquaintance who would vouch for me, but I'm already late for a meeting at the People's Education Committee. Today they're considering a proposal for a Polish Theater to be organized by the famous Polish actress Stanislawa Wysocka.

■ □ ■

When I walked into the Committee room, some twenty people had already gathered, including my former drama school teacher, Vladimir Sladkopevtsev. Wysocka was describing the theater she had in mind and her work plan. Since there were no Polish actors (professionals) in Kiev, the troupe would consist of young amateurs. The plays would be performed in Russian, but the repertoire would be exclusively Polish.

The floor was opened to questions. Sladkopevtsev, who was sitting next to me, pointed out a tall, slightly hunched man in a winter coat and a large hat that covered half his face: "That's Krzhizhanovsky." It was hard to make him out, especially as he was sitting in a dark corner.

■ □ ■

Every new literary work to reach Kiev from Moscow excited enormous interest. People would copy it down, recite it, debate it. The end of 1920 saw the arrival in Kiev of Blok's poem "The Twelve." It was all anyone wanted to talk about. Nothing conveyed better or more vividly that mood of confusion, that plunge into the unknown, that thirst for holy madness peculiar to the fury of revolution. One wanted to recite endlessly aloud, to sing out the poem's first lines—simple, yet charged with vitality:

> Black night,
> White snow.
> Wind O wind!
> It knocks you down as you go.
> Wind O wind—
> Through God's world blowing.[3]

Not long before, I had seen something that now kept coming to back to me, especially when I read the lines "But where is Katya? Katya's dead. A bullet through her head."

Walking out the front door early one morning into the yard, I noticed some twenty paces off a crumpled figure. In the yard there was a large round flowerbed enclosed by a low wrought-iron railing. The figure lay with its head against the railing. When I came closer, I saw that it was a woman in a faded cotton dress with a kerchief over her shoulders. She lay motionless, her head thrown back, knees bent, by her spine a small pool of blood. There was no doubt that she had been shot, most likely in the back. Her face was young, beautiful, with the regular features of many Ukrainian women, very serene, almost saintly. I stood over her corpse, not knowing what to do. Two or three more women approached, and soon a small crowd had gathered.

Death in those days did not affect most people. No one was in a hurry to find the murderer. Instead, remarks flattering and unflattering rained down on the woman: "That's Lenka from the laundry. Went too far"—was all I learned. But the image of that young, unfortunate woman haunted me. It blended strangely with the rhythm of the lines "Black night, White snow . . ."

I loved Blok before, but now he became especially dear to me; I owed my new sense of the times to him. For that reason, I was thrilled when Alexander Daich, a literary critic, suggested we put together a literary evening devoted to Blok. He would make the introduction, while the entire poetry section would be mine. I composed a program of my favorite poems, including "The Twelve."

It was early spring; the chestnut trees were in flower. The weather was warm and my heart full of joy, but also some fear: this would be my first such performance, and I didn't know if the audience would sit still for forty-five or fifty minutes of listening to poems.

I put all my faith in "The Twelve." I believed in it more than I did in myself. I wanted people to hear it, to know it, to accept it.

Literary and musical evenings then were gladly attended. The thirst for knowledge seemed insatiable. Everyone was studying something, wanted to remake something, to discover something new. Our evening, too, our evening of Blok, drew a large audience and met with great enthusiasm. During my reading of "The Twelve," the hall was sunk in that particular hush when there are no barriers between listener and performer.

At the end of the evening, Daich led me up to a very tall, thin, slightly stooped man with a pale nervous face: "Sigizmund Dominikovich Krzhizhanovsky would like to thank you."

Krzhizhanovsky shook my hand in silence. It was still light. The clocks had been moved ahead two hours, but after nine o'clock it was forbidden to walk in the street. Fortunately, Krzhizhanovsky and I were going the same way.

I was very happy then, but now I think that day was one of the happiest of my life. I was living in a time of great expectations, of unprecedented excitement; I had given my first public reading of Blok; and beside me walked a man about whom I had often wondered, a man whom I didn't yet know, but whose significance and charm I already sensed. And strangely, despite his somewhat forbidding reserve and aloofness, I wanted to take him into my confidence.

Krzhizhanovsky was already fairly popular in Kiev as a lecturer. He often appeared at the theater, or at the Conservatory with an introductory speech before a musical program. People said he was a brilliant speaker of enormous erudition, a bold and original thinker.

As we walked, I asked him, with some shyness, about his forthcoming appearances. He replied reluctantly and asked me about my plans. I, too, did not say much as I didn't know if I would perform again. At the time I was teaching scene practice at an acting studio. My performance that evening had been a fluke. Our conversation broke off. We walked on for a while in silence—and then, suddenly, we both began talking about the same thing and decided on the spot to give a series of literary evenings together. I left the choice of themes to Krzhizhanovsky and invited him to come round the next day to discuss our work in detail. My shyness had disappeared; it was easy both to speak and to be silent.

■ □ ■

Next day on the stroke of noon Krzhizhanovsky was sitting at the table in my room. In the daylight he looked even thinner and paler than he had the previous evening. We all suffered then from hunger and cold, but his gauntness and the bluish pallor of his face seemed sickly. Most performances were unpaid. Somewhat later, when conditions began to improve, performers were paid in kind—in groats, fruit jelly, and other foodstuffs. But at the time it was very hard. In my larder I had nothing but some apples given to me by a student who had just returned from the country. The apples were enormous, juicy, red. I offered one to Krzhizhanovsky, who later made fun of me, claiming that I had acted like Eve. That day we settled on our first program: Sasha Chorny and Andrei Bely.

■ □ ■

During our literary concerts I usually listened to the first part—that is, to Krzhizhanovsky's introduction. Little by little I gained a sense of his singularities as a lecturer, his method of presenting his material, and his techniques for affecting the audience. Krzhizhanovsky always thought in images and constructed syllogisms out of them. He would provide a logical sequence of striking images, then break the chain, allowing listeners to draw their own conclusions. When conversing with an audience or giving a lecture, he didn't range about the stage; his gestures were few, but expressive, his hands especially so, white with long thin fingers. He never used notes and quoted whole pages from memory. Yet there was always an element of improvisation; he was incapable of giving the same lecture twice. His low voice—slightly subdued, rich in overtones—captivated listeners with the unexpectedness of its intonations.

■ □ ■

Krzhizhanovsky and Bovshek began collaborating with a young composer, Anatoly Butskoi,[4] who served as their pianist. Together they presented a story by Chamisso, Peter Schlemihl.[5] *Butskoi had a high opinion of Krzhizhanovsky's intellectual and moral qualities; at the same time, he felt protective of him and worried about his hand-to-mouth existence.*

■ □ ■

"A man without a profession," Butskoi would say to me. "You understand, he has no profession."

Krzhizhanovsky had had a profession. He had studied law at the university, in tandem with classical philology. On graduating he was appointed assistant to a district attorney and had defended a few minor cases before revolution swept the old government and its laws away. He parted easily with his profession since by then he was giving all his energy and attention to literature and his own writing.

Butskoi had known Sigizmund Dominikovich for several years. It was from him I learned that Krzhizhanovsky was born in Kiev and raised in a Polish Catholic family. His father had served briefly in the military and then worked for thirty-five years as the bookkeeper in a sugar refinery. His mother, kind and intelligent, was very musical; she loved to play the piano and knew all of Beethoven's sonatas. Krzhizhanovsky was her youngest child and only son. Of his four sisters, the eldest, Stanislava, was already a well-known actress. The middle sister, Elena—beautiful, very feminine, in delicate health— was close to her brother, despite the difference in age. He felt at ease with her alone; to her alone he confided his plans and dreams. Married to the commander of a regiment, she had gone as a nurse to the front where he was fighting. Her husband was killed. Then her tuberculosis returned and she died. The other two sisters, Yulia and Sofia, had families of their own and no interest in their brother, whom they did not understand. Krzhizhanovsky returned their indifference. "Blood relations," he said, "aren't yet relations. They must pass an exam in kinship."

In the past three or four years Krzhizhanovsky had lost his father, mother, sister, and uncle—his father's brother, Pavel Aleksandrovich. This last death was a great moral blow. Krzhizhanovsky's uncle had seen something unusual in him, had valued his intelligence and many-sided abilities. He had a small estate near Kiev with a lovely garden in which he grew rare varieties of roses. This estate and a sum of money he had left to his nephew, but from his generosity there remained only an old wooden desk (which went into the stove to give some frozen people a little warmth) and a raw silk jacket. His uncle must have been fairly stout since the jacket flapped on Krzhizhanovsky, accentuating his thinness.

■ □ ■

Krzhizhanovsky taught at the Music and Drama Institute and at the Jewish Acting Studio, where he was much loved. One day the studio received a consignment of old clothes and shoes that someone had donated. It was suggested to Sigizmund Dominikovich that he apply for some part of it. He wrote: "For my talk on Glinka's roots, I ask a pair of boots; for my literary stance, a pair of pants." Before leaving for Moscow, he also managed to obtain from the studio a topcoat— very worn, of indeterminate color, but just his size.

■ □ ■

Krzhizhanovsky was such an exceptional phenomenon, I didn't try to divine the mystery of his selfhood. Still, our work on literary programs, frequent meetings, discussions, and debates gradually revealed certain aspects of his nature. I was drawn to his extraordinary nobility, his restrained intensity, his self-respect combined with an exceptional modesty. His nobility showed in the high-mindedness of his ideas, in his subtle understanding of art, in his attitude toward others. In conversation he never asserted his superiority for fear of offending or humiliating his interlocutor; he was always patient, always respectful of opinions and ideas not his own.

At the same time, he would not tolerate the least intimation of violence toward himself or others, however that violence might be expressed—in the realm of ideas or daily life. He was equally intolerant of lies and injustice. His face, while retaining its outward calm, would turn instantly pale; his eyes and lips would flash with a withering fire. He had thin nervous lips, sensitive to changes in mood and every shade of emotion—a true barometer of his soul.

MOSCOW

At the end of March [1922], Krzhizhanovsky arrived in Moscow with the Jewish Studio.[6] Before he left Kiev, friends had supplied him with several letters of introduction to Muscovites. His visit to Berdyaev with the first letter proved unsuccessful. From their conversation, it emerged that Berdyaev's philosophical and political positions were as insecure as his existence in Moscow.[7] The second letter, to Professor Avinov,[8] opened the door of that family's home to Sigizmund Dominikovich, but something kept him from pursuing the acquaintance further. He decided to pay no more useless calls. The third and last letter reposed for a long time unused in a side pocket of his jacket.

Then one day, in a small auditorium at Moscow University, as he was listening to a paper by Professor Ivantsov,[9] a sheet came around on which attendees were asked to write their names. Krzhizhanovsky signed and passed the sheet to the woman on his left: she wore a modest, dark suit and a serious, stern expression. She signed: L. B.

Severtsova. It was to her that the third letter was addressed. Ludmila Borisovna read the letter at once, introduced S.D. to her husband, Alexei Nikolaevich,[10] and proposed that after the lecture he come home with them to tea. The Severtsovs' apartment, in both S.D.'s life and mine, went on to play a very significant role.

It was there that we first met such remarkable academics as Vernadsky,[11] Zelinsky,[12] Fersman,[13] and Oldenburg.[14] It was there that we first heard a paper on the splitting of the atom and learned of new scientific developments.

Alexei Nikolaevich, a large, lumbering man resembling a fairy-tale bear, invariably affable and welcoming, took a somewhat dim view of art: "A nice, pleasant pastime, but one can live without it." Yet he loved literature, loved to listen to tales and fantastical stories; he would always ask me to recite something, only not too piteous; and in his leisure hours, he drew.

Ludmila Borisovna had been a student of his and married him after the death of his first wife. Much younger than A.N., she was closer to our age and sought us out. "A kind, frank, sweet person," S.D. said of her.

For him she immediately found a room: unfurnished, small, six meters [65 square feet], belonging to Count Konovnitsyn. The count did not ask money for it, but proposed that he take paid English lessons from his tenant. The conditions suited Krzhizhanovsky, who promptly lugged his things to Arbat, 44, Apartment 5. The lessons did not go on for long; the old count soon sickened and died; the countess moved elsewhere.

With the arrival of its new inmate, the room began to assume a habitable appearance. It now contained a wooden bed with horse-hair mattress, a plain deal table with two drawers, an armchair with a hard seat, and on the opposite wall—bookshelves. A handmade cloth and counterpane covered table and bed. Several photographs on the walls and two watercolors signed "M. Voloshin" completed the more than modest decoration. So the room remained to the end of Krzhizhanovsky's life.

■ □ ■

Krzhizhanovsky was a passionate traveler. He always brightened on a journey. He would stride about with a brisk confidence, his high head thrown back, gazing into the distance. Before departing for an unfamiliar place, he would make a thorough study of its geography and history, its cities, historical sites, and monuments, and if that place were abroad, then also the language. Before his arrival in Moscow, he had not made the necessary preparations and so decided to take the city by storm, in battle. He had the time and, never sparing the soles of his only pair of already shabby shoes, strode about Moscow, covering fifteen to twenty kilometers a day, from one end of the city to the other. He liked Moscow, and liked the process of mastering it.

■ □ ■

These regular rambles colored many of Krzhizhanovsky's Moscow writings ("Autobiography of a Corpse," "Quadraturin," "The Bookmark," "Seams," "Someone Else's Theme," "Red Snow," "Unwitting Street"), most of all "Postmark: Moscow." This long philosophical essay, along with an installment of Bulgakov's White Guard, *appeared in* Rossiya *(1925, no. 5), a literary journal founded and edited by Isai Lezhnev.*

■ □ ■

S.D. could easily dash off fifty thousand words in a few days and then suffer for weeks from his inability to squeeze out even a line. Yet during those torturous "creative voids," he went right on conceiving new ideas, without respite. His mind was always working—whether he was lying on the sofa, staring with wide eyes into space; or striding about the streets of Moscow; or sitting some quiet evening—intent, lost in thought—on a boulevard bench.

A subject would be set down on paper only after it had been painstakingly thought out, after the system of images and the story's structure had been determined, the right words found, the phrases polished. At first S.D. wrote in longhand, but gradually he fell into the habit of dictating his work. He needed to think aloud, to apprehend his text in the spoken word. He did not own a typewriter and never even considered buying one for his personal use.

■ □ ■

Krzhizhanovsky had arrived in Moscow with the manuscript of his Fairy Tales for Wunderkinder. *The gist of several of these tales was relayed to Alexander Tairov, founding director of the Kamerny Theater, who asked to meet the author. Tairov hired S.D. to teach a course in art history at his Experimental Studio.*

■ □ ■

Tairov's regard for Sigizmund Dominikovich grew, evolving over the years into a touching, almost tender solicitude for him. Once when

Krzhizhanovsky was in a difficult situation, Tairov became anxious: "Who is your worst enemy? Tell me. I have connections after all . . . Perhaps . . ." "No, Alexander Yakovlevich, I'm afraid not, nothing can help. I am my own worst enemy. I am that anchorite who is to himself a bear."

■ □ ■

Krzhizhanovsky continued to work with students, write new stories, and give readings, but his morale was low. Prerevolutionary publishing houses and associations were shutting down one after another. Krzhizhanovsky gave his *Fairy Tales for Wunderkinder* to the publisher Dennitsa, but it soon folded. Lezhnev accepted "Autobiography of a Corpse" for *Rossiya* but put off running the story—until the journal was forced to cut the number of its pages in half.[15]

Our finances were on the verge of collapse. Having no income for the summer, I went to stay with family in Odessa. On leaving Moscow, I didn't put much faith in S.D.'s assurances that things were looking up and that he was just about to receive a sure fee. My misgivings proved correct. Much as he tried to hide the bitter truth from me, it showed through in letters. The fee never materialized, and he became acquainted with "Dr. Schrott." That name was a synonym for hunger. In Germany, a doctor by that name had a sanatorium where patients underwent hunger cures. Playing with Schrott's name, S.D. tried to disguise the true state of affairs. He wrote: "The source of all my sorrows is rotten literary luck . . . [Still] it's either the way I want, or no way at all. I may be an aging, even slightly ridiculous fool, but my foolishness is so much mine that for it I feel both shame and love, as a mother does for her deformed child. And to hell with all that 'literature' . . ." And further on: "Though Dr. Schrott follows me about, I deftly manage to avoid meeting him face-to-face . . . I do wish that old man would give me the slip, or lose my address."

I read S.D.'s letters, and my imagination tormented me. Day and night I pictured him: sitting on a boulevard bench or in a park. It's evening. He loves the city and loves to be alone amid the noisy, scurrying crowds . . . Suddenly he feels that someone has sat down beside him. A little old man with a gray Vandyke beard, wearing a pince-nez on a long cord and a soft felt hat. Dr. Schrott. Smiling, the doctor proposes something to him. Krzhizhanovsky gets up, walks off, and keeps walking . . . pursued by Schrott.

■ □ ■

Deliverance came from Sergei Mstislavsky,[16] thanks to whom S.D. was hired as an editor[17] at the Great Soviet Encyclopedia. *And that winter Tairov decided to stage Chesterton's* The Man Who Was Thursday, *dramatized by Krzhizhanovsky.*

■ □ ■

The [nineteen] twenties and early thirties saw the full flowering of Krzhizhanovsky's talent. During those years he created such works as "The Collector of Cracks," "An Odd Man," "Seams," *The Letter Killers Club, The Return of Munchausen,* "Someone Else's Theme," "In the Pupil," and *Material for a Life of Gorgis Katafalaki.* But those years also brought him the greatest suffering. His manuscripts were invariably returned to him, sometimes with a polite, embarrassed smile and assurances that everyone on the editorial board had read it . . . very interesting, "but it's . . . not for us," other times without a word, defaced by a rectangular stamp with ten letters inside: DO NOT PRINT. Every "not for us" and "do not print" lay like a heavy weight on his brain, took his soul in a vise, filling him with pain, hurt, and bewilderment. Krzhizhanovsky was convinced that the reader needed him, that the reader would correct him in his mistakes, help him in his quests. For the sake of meeting his reader, he would have endured any privations, any trials whatsoever, but that meeting never took place.

He was in extremely low spirits in the summer of 1926 when he received a month's holiday from the Encyclopedia. He had to do something to pull himself together. He decided to make use of an invitation from Maximilian Voloshin[18] to come for a rest by the Black Sea at Koktebel: "Every day I go bathing and scorch myself. I'm not forcing myself to work: sitting by the sea and listening to the surf is far more interesting than fiddling with words." He described Maximilian Alexandrovich as an extremely interesting person, "a charming combination of wisdom and naiveté. Enormous and roaring, he reminds me of Sunday,[19] surrounded by us: the arriving and departing days. Again I'm the man who was, who knows, perhaps Thursday."

The guests at Koktebel lived in small, disparate groups; in the evenings they met for tea. Sometimes they gave readings. Krzhizhanovsky read too, and fairly often, always with success. About one reading, he wrote: "Your letter arrived just in time, a few minutes before I was to read. I calmed down and easily mastered the text. My story made a much stronger impression than might have been expected. When I finished, I saw myself surrounded by eyes staring intently and a good long silence. After which Voloshin, generally grudging in his praise, declared the story marvelous and merciless."

Before S.D. left Koktebel, Maximilian Alexandrovich presented him with one of his watercolors as a memento. He had inscribed it: "To dear Sigizmund Dominikovich, collector of the most exquisite cracks in our fissured cosmos."

But even Koktebel could not give Krzhizhanovsky complete peace. A second summer there was full of anguish and cravings for a change of scene and impressions. "Even here I cannot clamber out of my feeling of exasperation and bitterness. The breezes cannot sweep out, the sun cannot burn out the vile spume in me of that senseless and furious 'for what?' to which no intelligent person should listen."

■ □ ■

You couldn't say that Krzhizhanovsky was unlucky in his friends. His charm drew many people to him, though he found it hard to become close; his established friendships he valued and protected as sacred. Very demanding of himself, he was equally demanding of his friends. "Your friends are the ones you love, forgiving them nothing." Some, unable to withstand this test of friendship, drifted away. Which was always painful. In the difficult [nineteen] twenties, S.D. received moral support and help in literary matters from Mstislavsky, Levidov,[20] Lann,[21] and Antokolsky.[22] Lann and Antokolsky introduced him to Evdoxiya Nikitina,[23] organizer of the well-known literary circle "Nikitina's Saturdays."

Krzhizhanovsky gladly began attending Nikitina's Saturday meetings. She soon suggested that he present some of his stories. At various times he read "The Collector of Cracks," "The Branch Line," "Thirty Pieces of Silver," and chapters from *The Return of Munchausen*.

After one such reading, Nikitina asked Krzhizhanovsky to wait until the other guests had gone as she needed to speak to him. I felt awkward and afraid of being in the way, but the conversation took place in the next room. The reading had been a success, and although I knew that nothing could be wrong, I felt terribly anxious. By the look on Krzhizhanovsky's face when he appeared in the door-way, I understood that their talk had had a positive result.

Having said our good-byes, we walked down the stairs and out into the street. The house in which the meetings took place was on Tverskoi Boulevard, almost opposite the Kamerny Theater. We set off along the boulevard. It was late, with few people about. When we reached Timiryazev's statue, we sat down on a bench. I wanted to talk and talk. "What did she say? And then what did you say?" and so on. Nikitina had proposed that Krzhizhanovsky submit one of his theoretical works, "The Poetics of Titles,"[24] to her publishing cooperative. It was almost sure to be accepted since her vote was the deciding one.

The boulevard was deserted; now and then a late-night tram came clanging through the hush; a long shadow stretched from Timiryazev almost to our feet. We became carried away with a favorite dream of S.D.'s. He passionately hoped to visit England. While at work on *Material for a Life of Gorgis Katafalaki*, he pored over a map of London, studying the streets, the tangles of lanes, the squares and old statues with such diligence, he must have known them at least as well as longtime residents of that astonishing city. Now he told me that we would go to England, he would take me around the familiar streets of London, he would show me Westminster Abbey, Trafalgar Square, and other marvels.

The air was turning chilly; we got up and quickly set off along the boulevard. It was already very late when, having walked me home, Krzhizhanovsky returned to his room on the Arbat.

■ □ ■

[1930] Collectivization of Soviet agriculture had begun. Better-to-do peasants were driven out of their villages. Of the poor and middling ones, some abandoned their farms of their own accord; others remained but refused to work. Fields stood untilled and unsown; standing crops rotted on the vine. Hunger, having spread from village to city, ran rampant through the country.

In shops the shelves were again empty, while their windows displayed, in place of foodstuffs, copies of still lifes by famous Dutch masters in gilt frames. Black bread was rationed.

In offices, the staffs were being purged. People, fearing for themselves and their families, tried to avoid one another; they began destroying letters, books with inscriptions, photographs.

I could not stop worrying about Sigizmund Dominikovich. We lived apart and usually met in the evening. In the morning I never knew how the night had gone, if he had woken up in his own bed. Sometimes, unable to wait until evening, I would call the [Encyclopedia's] editorial offices after three o'clock, when I knew that work was winding down and my call would not betray my alarm. And I would hear the words: "Krzhizhanovsky has already left"—after which I could calmly wait for our evening meeting.

The fate of his manuscripts caused me particular anxiety. He would correct the typescripts in my room and then leave them there. Almost all of them were on a shelf in my wardrobe, covered with a length of gold-embroidered black brocade (an ironic allusion to their literary nonexistence).

Sergei Mstislavsky, to whom I turned for advice about how best to protect the manuscripts, told me that his position was no more secure than S.D.'s and that he was always waiting, for come what may . . .

My anxiety reached a peak the morning I walked into the Theater Library—where I was working temporarily—to find that of the eight people on staff, two had been arrested.

When I came home, I sat for a long time at my table, then paced the room, thinking hard, and then, going to the shelf with the manuscripts, I flung back the brocade and made a sudden decision—an absurd, senseless decision, but, so it seemed to me then, the only one possible.

Our [communal] apartment was heated with wood; a shed for the wood had been allotted to the three tenants. I packed the manuscripts in a basket and went downstairs to the shed. I stowed the manuscripts on top of the woodpile and covered them with more logs. As I clicked the padlock on the shed door shut, I realized the absurdity of my venture. Late that night it began to rain. I listened to the drops drumming on the windowpanes and felt that even they were laughing at me. I imagined that the shed roof leaked, that the drops were slithering down between the logs and soaking the paper, that the letters were becoming blurred, that the manuscripts, like living beings, were shivering and bemoaning my foolishness. I didn't sleep all night. At first light, I went back down to the shed, repacked the manuscripts in the basket and crept back up to my room.

Fortunately, S.D. never learned of that absurd episode. I mention it now because the feelings that I experienced then were typical not only for me, but for most of my acquaintance.

Krzhizhanovsky evoked the mood of those years, the general despondency and wariness, in "Red Snow" and "Memories of the Future."

■ □ ■

Many times I tried to persuade S.D. to come and live with me in my fairly large comfortable room with my personal telephone. He always said that he needed a room of his own, that life in one apartment—with the inevitable petty troubles, the disgusting conditions—would destroy the enchantment of friendly relations, kill the poetry of feeling. To dream of meeting was, to his mind, also a joy, sometimes no less a joy than the meeting itself. As much as he pined when we were apart, he defended the good side of such separations: they purified the image of the one cherished. Only at the end of his life, when he was dangerously ill, did he come to live with me—and still he kept his room on the Arbat.

More than anything, S.D. disliked and distrusted beautiful phrases and shows of emotion. On those rare occasions when he spoke of what he most prized—his country, literature, art—he was strict and exacting in his choice of words. He was equally reticent in his private life. He once gave me an English-Russian dictionary. On the title page, he had written: *See pp. 262, 572.* Turning to the pages noted, I read the words underlined—*darling, love.* Avoiding the usual timeworn expressions, Krzhizhanovsky carefully guarded his feelings, cloaking them in the words of another language. I was reminded of Chekhov: evidently obeying this same inner need just before he died, he said in German: "*Ich sterbe.*"

Difficulties began at the office. [The Encyclopedia's editor-in-chief] Schmidt,[25] away on another expedition, had left Lebedev-Polyansky[26] in charge. A heartless man of limited intelligence and no imagination, Lebedev-Polyansky was also scared. Everywhere in the work of his fellow editors he imagined he saw errors in ideology; he treated colleagues like functionaries. Krzhizhanovsky he did not trust. He found his work especially suspect and plagued him with absurd cavils. The situation was becoming harder and harder. S.D. decided to quit. After yet another cavil, he submitted a letter along these lines:

"Given that the experiment to turn me from a person into a functionary has not on the whole succeeded, I ask to be relieved of my duties as control editor."[27]

■ □ ■

Krzhizhanovsky left the Encyclopedia in early 1931 only to find himself in danger of being banished from Moscow as a "nonworking element." He told the police he was a writer. The police gave him three days to produce a certificate to that effect. Nikitina came to Krzhizhanovsky's aid: she quickly collected the recommendations necessary for him to be admitted to a Moscow writer's union; to reinforce that "writerly status," she rushed "The Poetics of Titles"[28] into print.

■ □ ■

The heroes of Krzhizhanovsky's stories do not have striking, complex personalities: their author needs them as semantic images to be put into play. But neither are they stick figures. They are living people who think and act with passion, with exceeding intensity. "Emotion in a thought," Krzhizhanovsky wrote, "is the overtone in a tone." The language of his characters resembles that of their author, who, having distributed the roles among his players, closely watches the progress of their intellectual battle. This battle does not require descriptions of daily details: the portrayals of actual conditions are as terse as those of characters' personalities. "I am interested not in the arithmetic, but in the algebra of life."

The devices favored by Krzhizhanovsky include hyperbole, irony, paradox, and phantasm. "A fantastical plot is my method," he wrote. "First you borrow from reality, you ask its permission to use imagination, to deviate from actuality; later you repay your debt to your creditor—to nature—with a doubly strict adherence to facts and an exact logic of conclusions."

It was to the logic of his conclusions that Krzhizhanovsky attached the greatest importance: "I'm not alone. Logic is with me."

Tolstoy said that the hero of his stories was Truth. About Krzhizhanovsky you could say that the hero of his stories was Thought, living human thought, the progenitor of all material and spiritual culture, thought come to life, falling, rising, wavering, but always pointing to the light, as a compass needle always points to the north.

■ □ ■

[1932] Ten years had passed since Krzhizhanovsky's move to Moscow. During that time he had written dozens of stories and novellas—including *The Return of Munchausen, The Letter Killers Club*, "Someone Else's Theme," and "Seams"—yet his literary life remained as unsettled as ever. With bitter irony, he could write in a notebook: "I am known for being unknown."

He continued to read new stories to a small circle of friends; his head teemed with new themes that he chased away ("No Vacancy"); he went on stubbornly and confidently dictating, but now appeared in the offices of publishers only rarely.

His finances were in a bad way, his spirits dismal. "Owing, evidently, to some clumsy mental movement, I have dislocated my self from myself, and now everything somehow irritates me . . . What's more, instead of reacting outwardly, letting off steam, I react inwardly. That is, I poison myself with utterly-unworthy-of-a-thinking-person bunk."

Once again during that difficult period of penury and stagnation, a friendly hand reached out to him. This time it was the hand of wise, honest, kind Levidov. It was Levidov who convinced Krzhizhanovsky that he needed to work on a wide front: if not here, then there he would achieve something. It was Levidov who made Krzhizhanovsky take up the study of Shakespeare.[29] It was he who supported S.D. morally and materially when he was working on his comedy "The Priest and the Lieutenant."

An ebullient and energetic man of sparkling wit and unfailing optimism, he had a tonic effect on his charge. S.D. wrote to me: "Levidov, with extraordinary tact and solicitude, almost like a nursemaid, fusses over me. Once every two or three days, at his insistence, I look in on him, and he always finds words of encouragement. Even when he talks about other things, he does so in such a way that I leave feeling cheered and calmed . . ."

■ □ ■

Krzhizhanovsky went on writing. He could not not write, just as a bee cannot not lay up honey, even if the honeycomb has been taken away. Work was his salvation. He led a solitary life and avoided people. Encounters for him were painful. He felt like a played-out player, a failure. He was ashamed of his role, yet he never ceased to believe in his creative possibilities and the usefulness of his work. He found the company of writers especially onerous.

[In the spring of 1940] the Lanns obtained for him a free twelve-day pass to a writers' retreat in Golitsyn. Krzhizhanovsky refused to go, but finally yielded to his friends' entreaties. On the tenth day, he fled. He had a good room and everything he needed for work, but the atmosphere oppressed him. "They don't tell me so," he complained, "but they perceive me as a sort of phantom, an apparition from literature. Though hardly a frightening one. I turn up for tea, for dinner, then evaporate behind the door of room № 8."

Neither his waking nor his dreaming hours gave him peace. Alcohol became a necessity. When asked what had brought him to wine, he joked: "A sober attitude toward reality."[30]

■ □ ■

Krzhizhanovsky had been belatedly accepted into the Soviet Writers Union in 1939. Two years later his last collection, Stories of the West,[31] *passed the censor; it was being typeset for the publishing house Sovietsky pisatel*[32] *when, in June 1941, Hitler invaded the Soviet Union.*

■ □ ■

War . . . Moscow was almost unrecognizable. Windowpanes criss-crossed with white strips of paper, shops fronted with sandbags, streets barricaded. Faces were serious, intensely preoccupied. Hardly a quarter of the population remained: the Germans were rapidly approaching Moscow; residents were rushing to get out of the city. At night there were air raids: people killed, buildings destroyed.

They arrested Levidov, the most loyal, patient, and kindhearted of friends, Levidov, who firmly believed in the power of the Russian soul and the inevitability of our victory.

Friends and acquaintances, one after another, were leaving for the East: for the Urals, for Siberia.

Krzhizhanovsky decided to remain in Moscow. To the bewildered questions of those departing, he replied: "A writer must remain with his theme."

A year before the start of the war, the Bolshoi Theater had commissioned him to write the libretto for *Suvorov*,[33] an opera with music by Vasilenko. When the Bolshoi evacuated to Kuibyshev, it ceded the opera to Moscow's Stanislavsky Theater. Krzhizhanovsky decided to stay so as to maintain contact with Vasilenko,[34] who had gone to Tashkent, also to keep an eye on rehearsals and make any necessary adjustments to the opera's text.

(I too remained in Moscow, teaching creative elocution at the House of Pioneers—the only place, with schools closed, where children could still play and take lessons.)

Suvorov had its premiere in February [1942]. People worried that an air raid would interrupt the performance or stop it altogether, but it went off splendidly. The theater was packed with men in uniform: commanders and soldiers. Many scenes, especially those with simple folk, were greeted with furious applause. Only after the performance was over and spectators had left the cloakroom did the bombardment begin. Instantly the sky lit up with the beams of searchlights, then came the crackle of our anti-aircraft guns. The air raid did not last long; the circling Messerschmitts disappeared.

When S.D. and I crossed Gorky Street,[35] the sky was again clear. The stars shone as brightly as they usually did on a frosty winter night. The snow crunched under our feet, glittering with bluish sparks.

We walked along in silence, reading each other's thoughts without words. War had enveloped half the world, every one of us had loved ones at the front, and death might strike them at any moment . . . but there was also a higher truth, a higher justice, for which one must now fight. We, in our way, had joined that battle. For the first time it seemed to us that we were an integral part of our people, fighting for our country, for humanity. That's why we felt so light and exultant.

This was an optimistic tragedy . . . [36]

Suvorov ran all through the war years, playing to full houses. To entertain soldiers in the city and at the front, a Suvorov Brigade was organized out of the opera's singers. As a member of that brigade, S.D. gave readings of scenes from *Suvorov* and sometimes from "The Priest and the Lieutenant."

■ □ ■

In the fall of 1942, Krzhizhanovsky was sent by the Theater Workers Union to Irkutsk, Novosibirsk, and Ulan-Ude to confer with stage directors there. "The conditions are nothing special (for instance, this is my third day without bread—such is the local administrator's 'good management'), but to hell with them, with the conditions," he wrote Bovshek.

"The main thing is to load up my brain with Siberian impressions, to remain in all ways and always a writer, to restock my 'coffer of images,' to treat the present as one does the past."

■ □ ■

Krzhizhanovsky returned to Moscow brimming over with impressions. Pale, utterly emaciated, he looked like the Krzhizhanovsky I first knew in Kiev. Except that now his hair was completely gray, the doleful lines around his mouth were deeper, and his eyes still warmer. I had rarely seen him so kind and lighthearted.

■ □ ■

Krzhizhanovsky would write another libretto and more essays, but no more fiction. By war's end he was weak and unwell. The universally shared hope that life in the victorious Soviet Union would become freer was quashed by fresh waves of arrests. Krzhizhanovsky went back to teaching at the Kamerny Theater school, but his lectures had lost their brilliance. He married Bovshek (October 15, 1946) and finally went to live with her.

■ □ ■

In his notebooks these lines appear:

"1. It's too late to think about life, it's time to consider my doom. 2. My life has been sung and sipped to the end. 3. My final destination is approaching—Death. It's time to pack up my ideas. 4. I must surrender my life as a sentry surrenders his post."

The first day of May [1950] was warm and bright, unusually so for Moscow. Out the window you could see a cloudless blue sky, people in light clothes and summer jackets.

Krzhizhanovsky sat in a deep armchair at the table, looking through journals. I lay on the sofa, reading. Suddenly I felt a stab in my heart, I looked up: he sat with a pale, frozen, frightened face, his head thrown back on the chair. "What's wrong?" I asked. "I don't understand . . . I can't read anything . . . A black raven . . . Black raven."

Clearly, something irreparable had happened . . .

The doctor said brain spasms had paralyzed the part of his memory that contained the alphabet. Krzhizhanovsky could write, but he could not read what he had written—he could not read at all. The manuscript of a translation he had just finished (volume 5 of Mickiewicz[37]) lay on the table, awaiting his corrections, but he could not read a single word. The doctor prescribed patience and rest.

Rest cures were not in Krzhizhanovsky's nature. He waited impatiently for his memory to return, but it would not return. He bought an alphabet and attacked it, trying to master the letters, but they would not be mastered.

At the end of October, he suffered a cerebral hemorrhage. During a moment of lucidity, I asked him: "Do you want to live?" He said: "I don't know. Sooner no, than yes." Then he quietly added: "If it weren't so banal, I would say that my heart is broken."

The psychiatrist from the polyclinic, wishing to form a picture of the disease, asked S.D. several questions. He replied reluctantly and incoherently. She knew that she was at the bedside of a writer. She asked him: "Do you like Pushkin?" "I . . . I . . . Pushkin." He began to cry uncontrollably, sobbing like a child, unashamed of his tears. I had never seen him cry before.

On the 28th of December, about four in the afternoon, he died.

Krzhizhanovsky surrendered his life as a sentry surrenders his post. He worked until the day disease struck his brain. And it is not his fault that all his hard life he was a literary nonbeing, honestly working for being.

1965

NOTES

INTRODUCTION

1. Sigizmund Krzhizhanovsky, *The Return of Munchausen* (1927–28), trans. Joanne Turnbull with Nikolai Formozov (New York: New York Review Books, 2016).

2. Between 2009 and 2020, five volumes of Krzhizhanovsky's prose fiction, translated by Joanne Turnbull with Nikolai Formozov, were published by New York Review Books. Alisa Ballard Lin is the translator and editor of his most ambitious play, *That Third Guy: A Comedy from the Stalinist 1930s with Essays on Theater* (Madison: University of Wisconsin Press, 2018).

3. See his 1937 sketch "Countries That Don't Exist," trans. Anthony Anemone, in *Countries That Don't Exist: Selected Nonfiction*, by Sigizmund Krzhizhanovsky, ed. Jacob Emery and Alexander Spektor (New York: Columbia University Press, 2022), 115–41, at 137.

4. "The Slightly-Slightlies," in *Unwitting Street*, by Sigizmund Krzhizhanovsky, trans. Joanne Turnbull with Nikolai Formozov (New York: New York Review Books, 2020), 19–28, at 20.

5. "In the Pupil," in *Autobiography of a Corpse*, by Sigizmund Krzhizhanovsky, trans. Joanne Turnbull with Nikolai Formozov (New York: New York Review Books, 2013), 31–60; "The Gray Fedora," in *Unwitting Street*, 68–80.

6. In one comedy, the young Soviet state, to improve its balance of trade, arranges to export its fools to the gullible West; in another, the fool is a disastrously bad poet and dupe of Cleopatra. For summaries, see Caryl Emerson, "Krzhizhanovsky's Collapsed Contributions to the Pushkin Jubilee," in Lin, *That Third Guy*, 269–92, esp. 272–76.

7. For an account of this "biographical library," see Ludmilla A. Trigos and Carol Ueland, "Creating a National Biographical Series: F. F. Pavlenkov's 'Lives of Remarkable People,' 1890–1924," *Slavonic and East European Review* 96, no. 1 (2018): 41–66.

8. See the final tale (chapter 6) in Sigizmund Krzhizhanovsky, *The Letter Killers Club* (1926), trans. Joanne Turnbull with Nikolai Formozov (New York: New York Review Books, 2012): 104–9; and "Bridge Over the Styx" (1931), in *Autobiography of a Corpse*, 151–61.

9. A. V. Sinitskaya, "Emblematicheskii printsip i prostranstvennye formy v tekste," *Literaturovedenie* (2003): 1–10.

10. "Idea and Word" (191?), trans. Timothy C. Langen, in *Countries That Don't Exist*, 15–28, at 25.

11. See "Shakespeare's Comediography" and "Fragments on Shakespeare" in *That Third Guy*, 161–235, 248–51.

12. "Edgar Allan Poe" (1939), trans. Joanne Turnbull, in *Countries That Don't Exist*, 143–48, at 144, 145, 146.

STRAVAGING "STRANGE"

1. A doctrine promulgated by the Pythagoreans that the celestial spheres are separated by intervals corresponding to the relative lengths of strings that produce harmonious tones (*Webster's Third New International Dictionary*).

2. Ever since going to work for a Soviet cooperative—the irony being that even a magus could not get out of Soviet Russia. (In this sense, he is perhaps a stand-in for Krzhizhanovsky, who longed to travel abroad after the Revolution, but never could.)

3. An old Russian measure of length, about two-thirds of a mile.

4. From tsarist Russia to Soviet Russia. In 1914, on a wave of World War I–inspired anti-German sentiment, St. Petersburg was renamed Petrograd; in 1924, after Lenin's death, Petrograd was renamed Leningrad.

5. An allusion to the hunger during the Civil War (1917–1922), when many Russians had to part with possessions in order to eat.

6. Boots that allow the wearer to take strides of seven leagues. They appear in European folklore, including Chamisso's *Peter Schlemihl* (1814).

7. A high mountain pass in the Swiss Alps.

8. An allusion to a Bolshevik slogan during the Russian Civil War, "Peace to the huts, war to the palaces!"

9. The Greek goddess of retribution or vengeance. She rewarded virtue and punished the wicked and all kinds of impiety (*Brewer's Dictionary of Phrase & Fable*, 16th ed., s.v. "*Nemesis*").

10. In the wake of the decimation of that Roman Catholic city on All Saints Day 1755, Kant produced papers on the causes of earthquakes and on their use; Voltaire wrote his "Poem on the Lisbon Disaster" (1756) and then used the event in *Candide* (1759) to dispute optimism.

11. Possibly an allusion to Aristotle's *Politics*, book 3, chapter 11: "The supreme power ought to be lodged with the many . . .: for, as they are many, each person brings in

his share of virtue and wisdom; and thus, coming together, they are like one man made up of a multitude."

12. The opening scene of Dante's *Inferno* (1321): he is lost in a savage forest, the Wood of Error, midway through life's journey.

13. The scene in *Macbeth* (act 5, sc. 4) where Malcolm's soldiers cut down boughs in Birnam Wood and bear them before them as they advance on the murderous king.

14. Hans Christian Andersen's "Ole-Lukøje" (1841), about a dream god who brings marvelous dreams to good children.

15. Count Alessandro di Cagliostro, the assumed name of Giuseppe Balsamo (1743–1795), an Italian adventurer and alchemist briefly embraced by the courts of Europe, England, and Russia.

16. An invented bit of hyperbole not to be found in the hyperbolic adventures of the semimythical Baron Munchausen. For the length of a verst, see note 3.

17. An allusion to those Russians who were stuck in the past after 1917, unable to adapt to the new life under Soviet rule.

18. "That *extraordinary* thing was a representation of endless duration, quite independent of any religious concept. At the said age [eight or nine], while I was pondering on eternity *a parte ante*, it suddenly came over me with such clarity, and seized me with such violence, that I gave out a loud cry and fell into a kind of swoon. A movement in me, quite natural, forced me to revive the same representation as soon as I came to myself, and the result was a state of unspeakable despair. The thought of annihilation, which had always been dreadful to me, now became even more dreadful, nor could I bear the vision of an *eternal forward duration* any better." Friedrich Heinrich Jacobi, *The Main Philosophical Writings and the Novel Allwill*, ed. and trans. George di Giovanni (Montreal: McGill-Queen's University Press, 1994), 362.

19. The five-year Russian Civil War that followed the Bolshevik coup in October 1917.

20. Nikolai Lyashko (1884–1953), whose 1922 sketch "Zheleznaya tishina" (Iron hush) evokes a once-booming ironworks reduced to silence and dereliction by the Civil War.

21. The Song of Solomon, a love idyll in the Old Testament.

22. Andrei Bely (1880–1934), poet and novelist, in his essay "Filosophia kultury" (The philosophy of culture).

23. A name invented by Swift (and later applied to this genus by Johann Christian Fabricius), while the anecdote about the "tiny male" was invented by Krzhizhanovsky.

24. The First World War (1914–1918) and the Russian Civil War (1917–1922).

25. The servant of Don Giovanni in Mozart's eponymous opera (1709). In his catalogue aria, Leporello lists, country by country, the many conquests of his libertine master.

26. Gottfried Wilhelm Leibniz (1646–1716), a German philosopher who attempted to reconcile the existence of matter with the existence of God.

27. Pierre Coste (1668–1747), a French publisher of Montaigne and translator of Locke.

28. The theory that matter alone exists.

29. A dark forest full of tangled thickets where the souls of suicides are trapped in gnarled trees: when their branches are broken, the trees bleed and speak (*Inferno*, Canto XIII).

30. 1 Samuel 17: 49–51.

31. Roman politician (d. 493 BCE), who in 494 BCE persuaded the plebs not to revolt against the patricians with this fable: "It once happened," he said, "that all the other members of a man mutinied against the stomach, which they accused as the only idle, uncontributing part in the whole body, while the rest were put to hardships and the expense of much labor to supply and minister to its appetites. The stomach, however, merely ridiculed the silliness of the members, who appeared not to be aware that the stomach certainly does receive the general nourishment, but only to return it again, and redistribute it among the rest." Quoted in Plutarch's *Lives*, Dryden translation, Vol. 1 (New York: Modern Library, 2001), 294–95.

32. An invitation, at the end of the Orthodox funeral service, to approach the open coffin and give the deceased a farewell kiss.

CATASTROPHE

1. Immanuel Kant (1724–1804), the German philosopher born in Königsberg (East Prussia), sometimes called the "Sage of Königsberg."

2. A river that runs through Königsberg (now Kaliningrad).

3. Kant's *Universal Natural History and Theory of the Heavens* (1755).

4. *the starry heavens above us—the moral law within us*: From Kant's *Critique of Practical Reason* (1788): "Two things fill the mind with ever new and increasing admiration and awe, the oftener and the more steadily we reflect on them: the starry heavens above and the moral law within." Immanuel Kant, *The Critique of Practical Reason*, trans. Thomas Kingsmill Abbott (1788).

5. The three-part logical argument (major premise, minor premise, and conclusion). Here, Kant's thinking.

6. To earthly things.

7. The Greek philosopher (427–347 BCE) who held that phenomena (things as they appear to our senses) do not represent the true essence of things.

8. George Berkeley (1685–1753), the Irish philosopher who, as an idealist, believed that to be is to be perceived—that material things cease to exist when not being perceived by any mind or spirit. (*The Penguin Dictionary of Philosophy*, ed. Thomas Mautner. London: Penguin, 2000).

9. In his *Critique of Pure Reason*, Kant presents four antinomies: four pairs of thesis and antithesis. Kant resolves the antinomies by asserting that in each antinomy, one of the two conflicting statements can be thought to apply to phenomena

(things as they appear to us), the other to noumena (things as they are in themselves). (*Penguin Dictionary of Philosophy*)

10. That is, Romanticism. In emphasizing the imagination and emotions over intellect and reason, the movement was a reaction against Neoclassicism. (*Benét's Reader's Encyclopedia*, 3rd ed. New York: HarperPerennial, 1987).

11. An allusion to a Russian folk song that amassed many new verses after the revolutions of 1917. Of these, the best known was: "Hey, little apple, / Where are you rolling? / You're mine to gobble, / So stop your bowling!"

12. The plane of the earth's orbit extended to meet the celestial sphere. (*Webster's*)

13. An allusion to Hegel (1770–1831), who defined nothingness as "complete emptiness, complete absence of determination and content; lack of all distinction within." In *The Science of Logic*, trans. George Di Giovanni (Cambridge University Press, 2010), 59.

MATERIAL FOR A LIFE OF GORGIS KATAFALAKI

1. Said by Socrates as quoted by Plato in *Theaetetus*.

2. "By the sea, by the desolate nocturnal sea, / Stands a youthful man, / His breast full of sadness, his head full of doubt. / And with bitter lips he questions the waves: / 'Oh solve me the riddle of life! / The cruel, world-old riddle . . . / Tell me, what signifies man? / Whence does he come? Whither does he go? / Who dwells yonder above the olden stars?' / The waves murmur their eternal murmur, / The winds blow, the clouds flow past. / Cold and indifferent twinkle the stars, / And a fool awaits an answer." From "The North Sea, Second Cyclus" in *Poems and Ballads of Heinrich Heine*, trans. Emma Lazarus (New York: R. Worthington, 770 Broadway; 1881), 215.

3. He confused the author of *Don Quixote* with Don Quixote's horse; the coauthor of *The Communist Manifesto* (1848) with the Great War poet, Gerrit Engelke (1890–1918); what there can be no knowledge of with the necessary presuppositions of knowledge (in Kantianism); and an eighteenth-century German philosopher with a nineteenth-century French one.

4. Johannes Ranke (1836–1916), a Munich-based physiologist and anthropologist who specialized in the forms of the human skull; author of the two-volume *Der Mensch*.

5. The slight projection occasionally present on the edge of the external human ear. (*Webster's*)

6. The state of exhibiting equal tendencies to growth in all directions. (*Webster's*)

7. Sir Henry Morton Stanley (1841–1904), a British explorer best known for his expedition into Central Africa to find the Scottish-born missionary David Livingstone (1813–1873).

8. The leaves of some tsarist-era tear-off calendars included suggested menus (e.g., for 22 February 1908: Blini with caviar—Fried fish—Blancmange).

9. Now Franz-Mehring-Platz.

10. A Roman Catholic devotion in honor of the Annunciation. It begins: *Angelus Domini muntiavit Mariae* ("The angel of the Lord brought tidings to Mary"). It is recited daily at the sound of the Angelus bell. (*Brewer's*)

11. A confused (Katafalakian) allusion to Schopenhauer's *The Art of Being Right: 38 Ways to Win an Argument* (1831). The thirty-eighth and last way involves not bullets but insults.

12. An inversion of the epithet ("the fearless and irreproachable knight") applied to the celebrated French Chevalier de Bayard, Pierre du Terrail (1473–1524).

13. A theatrical tale by the Italian playwright Carlo Gozzi (1720–1806) in which a fairy princess falls passionately in love with a mortal prince. As punishment, she is turned into a "monstrous serpent." But the prince, also passionately in love, kisses the serpent, which turns back into a fairy princess.

14. A one-act drama by the Indian writer Rabindranath Tagore (1861–1941) in which a princess (Chitra) asks the gods for perfect beauty to ensnare the warrior Arjuna— for a year. She succeeds, but soon regrets her deceit, while he feels that she is somehow hidden from him. When the year runs out and Chitra turns back into her true self, Arjuna says his life is full.

15. The assassination on June 28, 1914, of Archduke Francis Ferdinand of Austria by a Serbian nationalist that sparked the First World War.

16. From Hamlet's indictment of his faithless mother (act 1, sc. 2).

17. The Obry (as the Avars are called in the *Primary Chronicle*) are known for their conquest of the Slavic Dulebs in the seventh century and for their cruelty (they used Duleb wives in place of horses and oxen). The chronicle describes the Obry as "great in body and proud of mind"; for their pride, God destroyed every last one of them. Hence the Old Russian saying: "They perished like the Obrs." *Entsiklopedicheskii Slovar Brockhaus i Efron*, Vol. XXIa (St. Petersburg: 1897), 581.

18. Known before and after the Revolution for its public lectures.

19. Anatoly Lunacharsky (1875–1933), then head of the People's Commissariat for Enlightenment.

20. Polonius's sense of Hamlet's mental state (act 2, sc. 2).

21. Soviet Russia. The Bolsheviks wanted to jump straight from the tsarist past (feudalism) into the radiant future (socialism), bypassing capitalism.

22. The holsters of the two Cheka officials who arrived in a motorcar from Moscow, arrested Time, and took him away.

AFTERWORD

1. An Odessa-born Moscow Art Theater actress, Anna Bovshek (1889–1971) had studied under Stanislavsky, who stood in for her father at her marriage to a set designer in 1914. The next year she left the theater and her unfaithful husband for the war front, where she served as a Sister of Mercy. By 1920 she was living and working in Kiev.

2. John Scotus Erigena, ninth-century Irish theologian and philosopher.
3. In Alexander Blok, *The Twelve and The Scythians*, trans. Jack Lindsay (London: Journeyman, 1982).
4. A. K. Butskoi (1892–1965), a musicologist, director of Kiev's Music and Drama Institute (1920–1924).
5. Adalbert von Chamisso (1781–1838), a French-born German poet and botanist. Peter Schlemihl gives up his shadow to a tall gray man in exchange for an inexhaustible purse. Shunned by human society for his shadowlessness, he finds his only solace in nature.
6. Bovshek had gone ahead to Moscow and was staying with a friend, the actress Olga Preobrazhenskaya. Through her, Bovshek found a permanent room, in the apartment of Preobrazhenskaya's brother, at 3 Zemledelchesky Lane.
7. Nikolai Berdyaev (1874–1948), a religious philosopher, had been arrested in 1920 and briefly imprisoned. Rearrested in August 1922, he was forced into permanent exile abroad aboard the first "philosophers' ship."
8. Evidently Nikolai Avinov (1881–1937), an economist and former Kadet whose apartment at Povarskaya 18 was then under surveillance by the GPU. He had been holding secret meetings of fellow professors and former Kadets to discuss such topics as monarchism and the consequences of the Revolution. Arrested in 1931 and sentenced to three years in camp, Avinov was rearrested in 1937 and executed.
9. Nikolai Ivantsov (1863–1927), a zoologist who taught at Moscow University.
10. A.N. Severtsov (1866–1936), a biologist and founder of the Russian school of evolutionary morphology.
11. Vladimir Vernadsky (1863–1945), a founder of geochemistry and biogeochemistry, author of *The Biosphere*.
12. Nikolai Zelinsky (1861–1951), a chemist and Soviet academician.
13. Alexander Fersman (1883–1945), a geologist and Soviet academician.
14. Sergei Oldenburg (1863–1934), an orientalist and authority on Buddhist texts, a former leader of the Kadet Party and Minister of Education in the Provisional Government of 1917.
15. Lezhnev's *Rossiya* was banned altogether in March 1926; he was arrested and sent into exile abroad.
16. S. D. Mstislavsky (1876–1943), a writer who in 1918, as a commissar in the Red Army then occupying Kiev, had come across a tall, gaunt sentry reciting Virgil (in the original): his first encounter with Krzhizhanovsky.
17. In the Literature, Art, and Language section.
18. M. A. Voloshin (1877–1932), a poet and painter who, after the Revolution, turned his house in the Crimea into a government-sanctioned retreat for writers and artists.
19. President of the Central Council of Anarchists, whose seven members each assume a day of the week as an alias, in Chesterton's *The Man Who Was Thursday*.

20. Mikhail Levidov (1891–1942), a journalist and writer associated with *Izvestiya* under Bukharin and with Academia Publishers under Kamenev; author of a book on Swift.

21. Evgeny Lann (1896–1958), a writer, poet, and Dickens specialist.

22. Pavel Antokolsky (1896–1978), a poet, playwright, and stage director.

23. E. F. Nikitina (1895–1973), a critic, editor, and friend of People's Commissar Anatoly Lunacharsky, an honorary member of her literary salon (*Nikitinskie subbotniki*); she also ran an independent publishing cooperative.

24. A thirty-two-page monograph; the only stand-alone work of Krzhizhanovsky's to be printed in his lifetime. It appeared in 1931, the same year Nikitina's publishing cooperative was liquidated.

25. Otto Schmidt (1891–1956), a mathematician, astronomer and Arctic explorer.

26. Pavel Lebedev-Polyansky (1882–1948), head of the state censorship agency Glavlit, in which capacity he had vetoed Krzhizhanovsky's novella *The Letter Killers Club* in 1928.

27. A senior position, just below that of editor-in-chief. Control editors edited Encyclopedia entries and checked them for errors of fact, meaning, ideology, style, etc.

28. Translated by Anne O. Fisher in Sigizmund Krzhizhanovsky, *Countries That Don't Exist: Selected Nonfiction*, ed. Jacob Emery and Alexander Spektor (New York: Columbia University Press, 2022).

29. For a selection of S.D.'s essays on Shakespeare, see Sigizmund Krzhizhanovsky, *That Third Guy: A Comedy from the Stalinist 1930s with Essays on Theater*, trans. Alisa Ballard Lin (Madison: University of Wisconsin Press, 2018), 161–251.

30. This is the same explanation offered by the alcoholic narrator of Krzhizhanovsky's "Unwitting Street" (1933).

31. This title, proposed for purposes of camouflage, replaced Krzhizhanovsky's own: *The Unbitten Elbow*.

32. Publishing arm of the Soviet Writers Union.

33. Alexander Suvorov (1730–1800), a Russian military leader under Catherine the Great; undefeated in over sixty engagements, he was put on a pedestal during the Second World War.

34. Sergei Vasilenko (1872–1956), a composer and conductor.

35. Now Tverskaya Street.

36. An allusion to *An Optimistic Tragedy*, a play (1933) by Vsevolod Vishnevsky about a heroic woman commissar during the Russian Civil War; she quells the anarchy aboard a Red Navy ship only to be killed by accident. Tairov dedicated his production of this socialist-realist drama to the fifteenth anniversary of the Red Army.

37. The final volume (political writings, letters) of a Collected Works of the Polish Romantic poet Adam Mickiewicz.

R

RUSSIAN LIBRARY

Between Dog and Wolf by Sasha Sokolov, translated by Alexander Boguslawski

Strolls with Pushkin by Andrei Sinyavsky, translated by Catharine Theimer Nepomnyashchy and Slava I. Yastremski

Fourteen Little Red Huts and Other Plays by Andrei Platonov, translated by Robert Chandler, Jesse Irwin, and Susan Larsen

Rapture: A Novel by Iliazd, translated by Thomas J. Kitson

City Folk and Country Folk by Sofia Khvoshchinskaya, translated by Nora Seligman Favorov

Writings from the Golden Age of Russian Poetry by Konstantin Batyushkov, presented and translated by Peter France

Found Life: Poems, Stories, Comics, a Play, and an Interview by Linor Goralik, edited by Ainsley Morse, Maria Vassileva, and Maya Vinokur

Sisters of the Cross by Alexei Remizov, translated by Roger John Keys and Brian Murphy

Sentimental Tales by Mikhail Zoshchenko, translated by Boris Dralyuk

Redemption by Friedrich Gorenstein, translated by Andrew Bromfield

The Man Who Couldn't Die: The Tale of an Authentic Human Being by Olga Slavnikova, translated by Marian Schwartz

Necropolis by Vladislav Khodasevich, translated by Sarah Vitali

Nikolai Nikolaevich and Camouflage: Two Novellas by Yuz Aleshkovsky, translated by Duffield White, edited by Susanne Fusso

New Russian Drama: An Anthology, edited by Maksim Hanukai and Susanna Weygandt

A Double Life by Karolina Pavlova, translated with an introduction by Barbara Heldt

Klotsvog by Margarita Khemlin, translated by Lisa Hayden

Fandango and Other Stories by Alexander Grin, translated by Bryan Karetnyk

Woe from Wit: A Verse Comedy in Four Acts by Alexander Griboedov, translated by Betsy Hulick

The Nose and Other Stories by Nikolai Gogol, translated by Susanne Fusso

Journey from St. Petersburg to Moscow by Alexander Radishchev, translated by Andrew Kahn and Irina Reyfman

The Little Devil and Other Stories by Alexei Remizov, translated by Antonina W. Bouis

The Death of Vazir-Mukhtar by Yury Tynyanov, translated by Anna Kurkina Rush and Christopher Rush

The Life Written by Himself by Archpriest Avvakum, translated by Kenneth N. Brostrom

The Voice Over: Poems and Essays by Maria Stepanova, edited by Irina Shevelenko

The Symphonies by Andrei Bely, translated by Jonathan Stone

Countries That Don't Exist: Selected Nonfiction, by Sigizmund Krzhizhanovsky, edited by Jacob Emery and Alexander Spektor

Homeward from Heaven by Boris Poplavsky, translated by Bryan Karetnyk

CPSIA information can be obtained
at www.ICGtesting.com
Printed in the USA
JSHW020204250323
39300JS00002B/2

9 780231 199476